CHOSEN

BOUND BY BLOOD BOOK 1

ALSO BY RICHARD FIERCE

DRAGON RIDERS OF OSNEN

Trial by Sorcery
A Bond of Flame
The Warrior's Call
The Coin of Souls
Wings of Terror
Eyes of Stone
Tooth and Claw
The Servant of Souls
Smoke and Shadow
The Dark Rider
The Song of Bones
Sword and Crown
Tides of Darkness
Wrath and Ruin
Tomb of Oaths

MARKED BY THE DRAGON

Curse of the Dragon
Scale of the Dragon
Egg of the Dragon
Call of the Dragon
Wrath of the Dragon
Sacrifice of the Dragon

CHOSEN

BOUND BY BLOOD BOOK 1

RICHARD FIERCE

Dragonfire Press

Print ISBN: 978-1-958354-82-7

Shaoing
Shinraha Mountains
Tatenagawa
Ikje
Dangju
Zhencheng
Woncheok
Jinseong
Taepo
Kimchon
Gangcheok
Posong
Legend
Capital
Shrine
City
Mountains

CHAPTER 1

Kai Lin was going to meet her dragon.

Chosen while she was still in the womb, she had long anticipated this moment, and also dreaded it. It should have been an exciting day, and although she was experiencing many emotions, elation was not one of them. She rubbed her sweaty palms on her gown.

"Don't fidget," Sho, her father, said softly.

"I can't help it," Kai replied.

"Leave the girl alone," her mother intervened. "She has every right to be nervous. It's an important day."

"I'm aware, Ryoko, but we haven't even entered the city yet."

Kai looked out the window of the wagon and watched the landscape pass. Her mother was right, she *was* nervous. She was leaving behind everything she had ever known for a future of uncertainty and endless war. It didn't make sense to her that both men and women were forced to be Chosen. Were it up to her, she would have taken a very different path, one less fraught with danger.

She hissed in a breath and grimaced as a lance of pain ran down the back of her skull. Clenching her jaw, she focused her attention on the swirling pattern sewn into her gown and waited for the agony to fade.

"Is it the headaches?" Ryoko asked.

Kai nodded slightly, afraid to make the pain worse.

Her mother looked at her father. "They're becoming more frequent."

"It has something to do with the ceremony," Sho answered, though Kai could tell by his tone that he was merely offering a guess.

The headaches had been rare when she was younger, but as she grew, they plagued her more and more. Now that they were headed to Ikje for the ceremony, the flashes of pain were almost like clockwork. The agony faded, and Kai unclenched her jaw.

"It seems a sorry reward for being Chosen," she said lamely.

Her parents exchanged looks, but neither one reprimanded her. Had they been in public, she knew they would have made a show of chastising her. Being Chosen was a great honor, and anyone who said otherwise was akin to a traitor.

The rest of the trip was uneventful other than Kai's steady stream of gasps when the headaches overtook her. She'd never before desired to die, but now, it was tempting to wish for the relief it offered.

The walls of Ikje came into view, and Kai marveled at the number of people who had come to attend the ceremony. Commoners and nobles alike crowded at the gates, eager to gain entry.

"We're here," her father announced.

Despite her anxiousness, Kai was curious to see the other Chosen. Were they nobles like her, or commoners? Or was there a mix? She would soon find out. The wagon trundled through a gatehouse, and guards lined the cobbled street, keeping the inquisitive at bay. That was one thing she disliked about being Chosen. She wasn't treated like everyone else. Instead, she had been kept in seclusion.

To say her childhood had been laborious was an understatement. She'd never been given dolls or other toys, had never played with another child. Upon asking about it, her parents only told her that being Chosen wasn't just an honor, it was also a sacrifice. She never understood that answer then, but she understood it now.

The wagon came to a halt, and the door swung open to reveal a soldier in leather armor. The faceplate of his helmet was missing, and his brown eyes swept over the interior, coming to rest on her. He was thin but muscular and had a stoic demeanor.

"Chosen," he greeted. "My name is Liu Wei, and I have been assigned as your personal guard. Please, follow me."

Kai stood and looked at her mother for assurance. Ryoko smiled at her, though her eyes were full of tears that threatened to spill and run down her cheeks.

"Everything will be fine," she said, rising to embrace her.

The words rang hollow in Kai's ears, but she knew her mother meant well. The lifespan of most Chosen wasn't very long, but that was to be expected when their job was to protect the kingdom from the incursion of the Drakka.

She'd had many nightmares of the terrible creatures, some so vivid she questioned if the dreams had truly been visions. The guard cleared his throat, and Kai lunged for her mother, embracing her tightly. She hugged her father next, and then she stepped out of the carriage and into an entirely new world.

Liu offered her a friendly smile and turned about, leading her across an expansive courtyard toward the castle. It towered above the city of Ikje like a sentinel, and flying overhead was a group of Sworn. Kai's breath caught in her throat at the sight of the mighty dragons soaring across the sky. Those riding upon their backs were too small to be seen clearly, but she knew they were there because their armor glinted under the sun.

Kai walked as fast as her short legs could go, but Liu was outdistancing her. He glanced back at her and slowed his pace.

"Apologies," he said. "I tend to walk fast."

Kai smiled sheepishly, but she didn't know why he was apologizing. Although she was born of a noble family, as one of the emperor's men, he likely outranked her. They reached two massive doors and at Liu's command, a host of guards scrambled to push them open.

Looking through the entrance, she saw a long hall with a vaulted ceiling. Globes of white light were spaced every six feet, and they hovered in the air of their own volition. Kai's eyes widened. She had seen magic before, but this was something much grander.

She looked over her shoulder, but her parents' wagon was gone.

Her heart hammered in her chest as panic started to overtake her, but she took a deep breath and reminded herself that she would see her parents again at the Ceremony of Oaths. Kai followed Liu inside, and the doors closed behind them. She gazed around the hall. The walls were bare of any decorations, which she found odd until she realized this area was part of the barracks.

"Where are we going?" she asked.

"To your personal chambers."

"I have my own room?"

"No. All of the Chosen have been assigned to the same room, but you will each have your own bed. I expect after the ceremony you'll be transferred to Dangju for training."

"I thought we were supposed to train here?"

"Normally you would," Liu replied, turning to the right and leading her down a new hall. "We've received reports that a large force of Drakka have been seen in the area, and the general feels that it would be safest to have you train elsewhere in the event they attack the castle."

Kai frowned. The Drakka had never attacked Ikje before. Between the emperor's soldiers and the Sworn, it was too well protected. She hissed in a breath and leaned against the wall, closing her eyes against the pain of another headache.

"Are you all right?"

"I will be," she whispered in reply. After the pain subsided, she opened her eyes to see Liu staring at her, his eyes full of concern. She pushed off the wall and stumbled, but Liu caught her. He placed a hand on her forehead. His touch was surprisingly gentle, and Kai felt a rush of warmth spread through her body.

"I get headaches," she replied. "They can be rather crippling."

"We're almost there," Liu said. "Just a little further."

He supported her with his arm, and they made their way slowly down the hall, stopping at a wooden door on the right. Liu pushed it open and helped her inside. The room was spacious, with several beds lining the walls. Each bed had a trunk at its foot, and Kai assumed that was where she would store her belongings.

"You can take the last bed on the left there."

Kai looked to where Liu pointed and saw a girl that looked to be her age lying on one of the beds. She wore a chainmail shirt and had her feet crossed, her dirty boots resting on the clean, white blanket that draped the bed.

"When is the ceremony?" Kai asked, looking at Liu. Despite her curiosity about the other Chosen, she didn't really want to be left alone with them.

"In a few days. We're awaiting the arrival of the dragons. Without them, there isn't much we can do. Should I call for a physician?"

"No, I'm fine. The pain comes and goes. There is nothing that can be done for it. My parents have tried everything."

"I see. I will leave you to rest, then."

"Wait. What do we do until the dragons get here?"

"Whatever you like, so long as you remain inside the castle."

"Are we prisoners?" Kai asked.

"Of course not. It is for your protection. If you'd like to go outside, I can arrange for an armed contingent to escort you around the grounds?"

Kai hesitated. The idea of being free to do whatever she wanted was foreign to her. Finally, she shook her head.

"No, thank you. I'll stay indoors."

"Excellent," Liu said, and Kai had the feeling he was glad he wouldn't have to organize a patrol for her. "Food and water will be provided every few hours. Unless you need anything, I shall take my leave."

Although she had just met the man, she considered him a friend and was hesitant to dismiss him. She reminded herself that she had no friends, and that he was only a soldier tasked with keeping her safe.

"I do not need anything," she said.

He smiled and bowed his head to her, then left the room. Kai stood in place awkwardly for a long moment, debating on whether to lay in her bed or wander around the castle. Pain clawed at the inside of her skull, and she decided lying in bed was the better option. She walked down the row of beds, glancing at the woman in the chainmail as she passed.

The woman cracked her eyes open and returned her stare, causing Kai to look away. She climbed onto her bed and laid down, surprised at how comfortable the mattress was.

"I'm Siran," the woman said.

Kai lifted her head and looked over at her. She had her eyes closed again, but somehow it felt as though the woman was watching her.

"I'm Kai."

"You look a little soft to be a Chosen. Are you a Chosen?"

"I am."

Siran grunted. There was a long pause, and then she said, "The others were in here earlier, but they went to explore the castle. That's commoners for you. Impressed with mundane things."

"How many others are there?" Kai asked.

"Ten, I think. I didn't really count them. The servants were whispering that we're the smallest group of Chosen they've seen in years."

Kai didn't know if that was good or bad, and she didn't ask. She fidgeted with the edge of her gown, running the material under her nails. It was a nervous habit.

"You're too loud," Siran said.

"I'm sorry."

"It was a joke. Actually, you're too quiet. Say something."

"Aren't you trying to sleep?"

"No. I'm listening to my dragon."

"What do you mean?"

"He's thinking. When he thinks, I listen. It helps me learn about him."

Kai was silent for a moment, debating on whether to speak her mind. Deciding she was tired of maintaining an illusion, she spoke up.

"What's it like? Hearing your dragon, I mean?"

CHAPTER 2

Siran sat up and looked at her. "What do you mean? You don't hear your dragon?"

"I don't think so. How would I know?"

"You would know, trust me. What *do* you hear? It should be a voice within your mind."

Kai always had a buzzing sound in her ears, and she long suspected it was related to her headaches, though whether it was the cause or a side effect, she didn't know.

"It's hard to describe, but there's a constant noise. Definitely no voice."

Siran frowned. "That's odd. I'm sure Master Satoshi will be able to help you."

"*The* Master Satoshi?"

"Yes."

Kai couldn't believe it. Master Satoshi was a hero. He'd saved the emperor's life—twice, and his list of accolades was long.

"Have you met him?"

"Not yet," Siran replied.

"Do you think the legends about him are true?"

"I'm sure there is truth to them, but like many things, they're probably exaggerated. I mean, they say he took out a dozen Drakka on his own. That's impossible."

Kai had heard that story before many times. Although she had never seen a Drakka in real life, she'd seen drawings of them. If they were anything like their illustrations, there was no way a single man could defeat an entire group of them.

"Anyway, where are you from?"

Kai hesitated before answering. She had been taught that it was unwise to reveal too much to strangers, but she decided since she'd be spending her foreseeable future with Siran and the other Chosen, it wouldn't hurt to be friends with them.

"I'm from the south. Woncheok."

"I've heard of it. Never been there, though. I'm from Posong."

"Where is that?" Kai asked.

"A week's journey southwest from Woncheok. There's nothing worth seeing there. Just farmland mostly."

"Are your parents farmers?"

Siran scoffed. "Hardly. My father is a Steward."

"So is mine."

"Thank the gods I'm not the only noble here. The others are all commoners." Siran frowned. "I don't know why they let them bond with dragons."

"It isn't up to us," Kai replied. "Dragons choose their riders."

Silence fell between them, and Kai closed her eyes. The constant buzzing sound was louder here, and the pain of another headache was coming. She tried to push it away, but it quickly overtook her.

"Are you all right?" Siran asked, noticing her discomfort.

"I will be," Kai whispered through clenched teeth.

"Do you need some water or something? Should I call for your guard?"

"No." Kai gasped in relief as the pain receded. "No, I'm fine. I get headaches sometimes."

"You should see one of the physicians about that. They can give you something for the pain."

"I've been to many of them before. Nothing helps."

"You might be surprised. I'll go with you if you want?"

Kai was caught off-guard by the woman's kindness. "I... suppose it wouldn't hurt to try."

"Follow me."

Siran led her out of the room and they traversed the hallways until they reached a large room with a high ceiling. The air was filled with the pungent scent of herbs and the low murmur of voices. Kai saw rows of beds, and some were occupied by patients in various states of health.

A gentle-faced physician sat at a wooden table, grinding dried leaves with a mortar and pestle. She looked up at Kai and smiled.

"Can I help you?"

The woman had a visage that was shaped by the passage of many years, and her white robes rustled as her wrinkled hands continued grinding away. Kai hesitated, unsure of what to say.

"She has headaches," Siran answered for her.

"Come, sit." The woman motioned to a stool beside her.

"I'll wait outside for you," Siran said. "All of this," she waved her around, "makes me uncomfortable."

Before Kai could reply, Siran turned and exited into the hall. Inhaling a deep breath, Kai walked over to the table and sat beside the woman.

"Tell me of your pain," the woman said.

"I get headaches, as she said. I've had them ever since I was young. They come on suddenly, and the pain is strong. Lately, they've gotten worse and more frequent, but every physician I've seen has been unable to help."

The woman nodded, her hands still working the mortar and pestle, but her eyes were focused on Kai. "Where do you feel the pain? Is it behind your eyes?"

"No," Kai answered. "It's near the back of my head, almost at my neck."

"I see. Lean closer. My eyes aren't as sharp as they once were."

Kai tilted her head toward the woman. She set her pestle down and placed a gentle hand on Kai's forehead. Kai felt a warm energy emanating from the physician's touch, and it soothed the faint lingering pain.

"Not all pain is of the flesh," she said cryptically.

"What do you mean?"

"There is a strange energy entwined within you."

"Are you talking about my dragon?"

"No." The woman offered no explanation. "Medicine may help you for a short time, but it will not solve your problems. You must seek the source of your pain from within and fix your *ki*. Only then will your headaches cease."

Kai blinked and furrowed her brow. The woman may as well have spoken in another language for all the sense it made.

"What do I need to do?"

"I cannot give you all the answers. I merely point you in the direction. You must do the rest."

The woman's ambiguous words were not particularly helpful, but Kai smiled anyway. Pretending was something she had grown accustomed to.

"Thank you," she said, rising from the stool.

"Take this. It will provide some relief, but only use it when the pain is unbearable. Consuming too much will dull your senses and cloud your mind."

Kai accepted a small pouch filled with herbs before returning to the hall. Siran was there waiting for her.

"Did she help you?"

"I'm not sure. She gave me this." Kai held up the pouch and Siran looked inside, wrinkling her nose.

"That stuff can be addicting. Try not to use it if you don't have to."

"That's what she told me," Kai replied.

As they walked down the corridor, the torchlight flickered against the stone walls. Kai clutched the pouch of herbs tightly, her mind replaying the physician's words.

"She said something I don't understand," Kai said, her voice echoing in the empty hallway.

"What?"

"Something about fixing my *ki*. She wasn't very clear."

"Your *ki* links you to your dragon, among other things. I don't know much beyond that. Maybe Master Satoshi will have more answers."

Kai hoped someone, anyone, would have some answers to a few of her questions. Most pressing of all, why couldn't she hear her dragon's voice if she was Chosen?

CHAPTER 3

When they returned to their bedchamber, the other Chosen were there. A chorus of voices filled the air, all of them talking excitedly.

"What did we miss?" Siran asked loudly.

"The Sworn have captured one of the Drakka. They're securing it so we can study it safely."

Kai looked at the one who had spoken. He looked to be about the same age as her, though he was taller by roughly a foot. He had dark hair that fell messily across his forehead, and his eyes were dark and hooded. She guessed by the deepness of his tan that he worked outside, probably in the rice fields. He met her gaze, then his eyes swept her up and down.

A chill ran down her spine at the intensity of his gaze, and Kai looked away. There was something about him that made her uneasy, though she couldn't quite pinpoint what it was. He seemed normal enough.

"I'm Ichiro," he said, introducing himself. "Nice to meet you, fellow Chosen."

"I'm Kai."

"Have you seen the castle grounds yet?"

"Briefly. I've only just arrived."

"I could show you around if you'd like?"

Before Kai could respond, another of the Chosen joined them, a disarming smile parting his lips. "Don't mind him. He's just looking for an excuse to get out of training duty."

Ichiro scowled. "Ignore Jiro. He's always putting his nose where it doesn't belong."

Jiro rolled his eyes, but Kai could tell the exchange was playful. The similarity between them was apparent, and their names made it obvious they were brothers considering Ichiro meant first-born son.

As the banter between Ichiro and Jiro continued, Kai found herself relaxing in their company. The tension that had been coiled in her shoulders since she arrived at the fortress began to unwind, and she even managed a small smile at their sibling rivalry. She decided to push aside her reservations.

"Do you still want to show me the grounds?" Kai asked.

"Of course. Let's go before Jiro convinces you that he gives better tours," Ichiro joked, earning a playful shove from his brother.

Kai looked at Siran, who remained standing quietly at her side. "Do you want to come with us?"

She thought the girl would decline, and was surprised when Siran shrugged.

"Sure."

The group set off through the labyrinthine corridors of the castle, passing bustling servants and nobles going about their business. Ichiro proved to be a knowledgeable guide, regaling Kai with tales of the fortress's history and pointing out hidden nooks and crannies where one could escape for a moment of solitude.

As they strolled through an open garden filled with fragrant blooming flowers, Kai noticed a figure standing at the edge of the garden, watching them with intense interest. The person was cloaked in shadow, their features obscured. Kai's breath caught in her throat, sensing a strange familiarity emanating from the mysterious figure. Before she could react, the person turned and disappeared into the shadows, leaving Kai feeling a sense of unease prickling at her skin.

"Did you see that?" Kai whispered to Siran, who shook her head.

"See what?" Ichiro asked, glancing around.

"Nothing. Never mind."

Ichiro continued the tour, but Kai couldn't shake off the feeling of being watched. She noticed fleeting glimpses of movement in the corners of her vision and heard whispers carried by the wind that seemed to speak her name. Each time she turned to investigate, there was nothing there.

They reached a secluded part of the garden, and Ichiro stopped and turned to Kai, a mischievous glint in his eyes. "There's a hidden passage here that leads to a lookout point with a stunning view of the valley. Care to see it?"

Kai hesitated. Despite knowing they weren't supposed to venture outside the castle, she felt the allure of rebelliousness. She'd spent her entire life living under the rule of law... what was one transgression? Besides, once she was Sworn, she may not live long enough to enjoy another moment like this. She nodded.

Ichiro led the way, and they filed into a narrow passage concealed by overgrown vines and moss-covered stones. The air grew cooler as they descended underground, the faint sound of dripping water echoing around them. The path sloped upward, and they emerged on the other side of the wall.

The dense canopy above cast dappled shadows on the ground, and Kai's unease heightened. The air seemed to grow heavier with each step they took. Ichiro continued guiding them, his steps sure and confident. The trees opened up to a clearing where a stone plateau overlooked the valley below. Ichiro walked to the edge of the plateau and gestured grandly towards the sprawling valley below.

"Behold, the lands we will protect once we are Sworn," he proclaimed.

As the rest of them stepped onto the plateau, a sudden gust of wind whipped through the clearing, causing the trees to sway and creak. Kai shivered, feeling a sense of foreboding creep over her. The view of the valley lay before them, and the sky was bathed in hues of orange and red by the setting sun. Kai stepped closer to the edge, her heart pounding in her chest as she took in the breathtaking scenery.

In the distance, she noticed something peculiar on the horizon. A dark cloud was rapidly approaching, billowing and churning in an unnatural manner. Fear prickled at the back of her neck, and she turned to the others with wide eyes.

"What is that?" she asked.

Ichiro's confident demeanor faltered for a moment as he followed Kai's gaze to the ominous cloud. His expression turned grim, his jaw clenching.

"It looks like a storm," he replied.

Jiro took a step back, his playfulness replaced with nervousness. "We should go back. Now."

Ichiro nodded, not bothering to argue. They retreated back through the damp, dark tunnel and a sense of urgency hung in the air. Kai's mind swirled with thoughts of the approaching storm. What kind of storm moved with such malevolence and speed? And why did it fill her with a primal fear she couldn't shake?

Emerging back into the garden, they were met with an eerie stillness that contrasted sharply with the chaos looming on the horizon. The once vibrant colors of dusk had faded into a somber palette as dark clouds gathered overhead, blotting out the last remnants of sunlight. A peal from the bell tower broke the stillness, a deep resonant tone that reverberated throughout the castle grounds.

"Let's get inside," Siran said, her tone full of authority.

Ichiro and Jiro sprinted off. It was obvious they were used to taking orders. Kai glanced up as rain began to patter around them, and she hurried to catch up to Siran. They entered the main hall and Kai noticed a hush had fallen over the fortress.

The servants moved with a practiced silence, their footsteps barely audible as they went about their duties. The nobles mingled and conversed in hushed tones, their words carrying an air secrecy. A group of Sworn passed by, their tense expressions hinting at the weight of their responsibilities.

"What's happening?" Kai whispered.

"I don't know... but we should probably be prepared for the worst."

CHAPTER 4

The strange storm laid siege to Ikje for two full days. The howling wind and relentless rain battered the fortress, causing water to seep through cracks and leak into the library. Kai and the other Chosen were forced to help the servants, who scrambled madly to staunch the flow. They mopped the floor and moved valuable tomes to safer areas.

The landscape outside the fortress fared worse. Ancient trees that had withstood all manner of ill weather burst into flames from lightning strikes, reduced to ruins in an instant. Rivers swelled and overflowed their banks, washing away shoots of grain that already struggled to grow.

When she wasn't helping the servants, Kai spent her time looking out the window. The ominous darkness that shrouded Ikje seemed to seep into her very bones, filling her with a deep sense of foreboding. As the hours stretched into days, whispers began to circulate among the castle that a curse had befallen Ikje, that a vengeful spirit was unleashed for some unknown transgression. Kai tried to dismiss these rumors as mere superstition, but she couldn't shake off the feeling of being watched, of unseen eyes following her every move.

On the morning of the third day, the storm abated. Kai awoke to someone pounding loudly on the door to their chamber. She sat up and looked around groggily. The other Chosen were slower to move. They were as exhausted as she was, and she didn't blame them for not wanting to stir. The door swung open, and Liu strode into the room, followed by a dozen other guards.

"Rise and prepare yourselves," Liu said. "Breakfast is ready in the dining hall, and once you have eaten, you will come to the dungeon to study the Drakka."

Kai's stomach turned at the thought of seeing one of the creatures in the flesh. The guards left, and the Chosen hurriedly dressed and made their way to the dining hall, where a simple meal of rice and bread awaited them. Kai ate in silence, her thoughts weighing heavily on her. She wondered how her parents had fared during the storm. No one had brought word that anything had happened to them, so she assumed they were well.

After their meal, Liu and the other guards led them to the dungeon. Torches flickered along the stone walls, and the air was musty and warm. The sound of dripping water echoed in the shadows, remnants from the storm.

The dungeon was a series of winding tunnels lined with prison cells. They continued onward until they reached a dead-end where a heavy iron door blocked the way ahead. Liu produced a set of keys and unlocked the door, then motioned for them to enter. Kai exchanged looks with the other Chosen before stepping across the threshold.

The room was well illuminated with spheres of white light that bobbed overhead. Several figures in blue robes trimmed in gold lined the walls, their complete focus on the hulking form in the center of the chamber. Chained to the stone floor was a creature unlike anything Kai had ever seen before.

It possessed a muscular frame with broad shoulders, and its skin was a green hue that glistened like wet clay. A mane of wild, jet-black hair cascaded down its back in tangled waves. The creature's visage was a grotesque mask of fury and malice. Two long, curved horns protruded from its head, sharp and gleaming like polished ebony. Smaller horns arced back from its shoulders, and its nose was broad and flat, nostrils flaring with each exhalation, while a wide mouth revealed rows of sharp, yellowed fangs that seemed designed to rend flesh from bone.

Adorning its powerful limbs were iron-studded bracers and anklets. Clawed hands, each digit tipped with talons as black as night, looked capable of crushing stone and tearing through armor with ease. Hanging loosely from its hips was a tattered loincloth, the only semblance of clothing it wore.

Kai felt her breath catch as she took in the sight. She had heard tales of the Drakka since she was a child—of their fearsome power and insatiable hunger for destruction. To be standing so close to one now sent a wave of dread down her spine.

Liu stepped forward, his voice steady but laced with caution. "This is our enemy. They are dumb creatures, but what they lack in wits they make up for in brute strength and viciousness. Note its green skin. Can any of you tell me what that signifies?"

"I can," Siran answered. "Green Drakka have power over the earth."

"Someone has spent some time studying," Liu said, sweeping his gaze over others. "Green are the most common, but there are others. For now, we will focus on this one. Drakka are strong beyond measure, but they are not invincible. Your dragon can easily dispatch one, but if you find yourself battling one alone, your best option is to strike here." Liu stepped closer to the beast and motioned to its chest. "A sharp blade to the heart will be sufficient."

The Drakka strained against the chains, and despite Liu's confident manner, he jumped back. The chains held, and the Chosen chuckled nervously.

"We have him bound," one of the robed men said. "He will not break free."

Kai turned her attention to the man. His blue robes indicated he was an Inquisitor, a soldier of the empire gifted with the power to control magic. Kai had never met an Inquisitor, but he seemed an ordinary man like any other.

Liu continued his lesson, pointing out the various weak points on the Drakka's body and how to defend against its brutal attacks. The Drakka shifted its weight, muscles rippling beneath its emerald skin. It seemed to radiate a primal energy that both intrigued and terrified Kai. She couldn't tear her gaze away from the creature, despite the unease churning in her stomach. The beast flicked its gaze back and forth from Liu to the Inquisitors. He'd said they were dumb, but Kai sensed the Drakka was studying them, calculating a way to escape.

"You all look terrified," Liu said, bringing Kai's attention back to him. "As well you should be, but soon you will no longer be Chosen. You will be Sworn, and as such, it is your duty to protect and defend the empire from them. Kai, come closer."

Kai's spine stiffened at the mention of her name. She met Liu's gaze, and he nodded slightly. He was tasked with protecting her, so if he didn't think there was any chance of the Drakka harming her, then she should trust him... shouldn't she? She swallowed hard and slowly drew closer to the creature.

It ignored her at first, but its nostrils flared, and it whipped its head toward her.

"Calm your fears," Liu instructed. "Match its gaze and let it know you are not afraid."

Kai looked up at the Drakka and met its stare. Her knees trembled, but she kept her face from contorting in fear. The creature sniffed the air once, twice, and then it leaned down, regarding her curiously. There was an intelligence in its eyes. She could see it clearly. Something inside her willed her to reach out her hand.

Hesitantly, she lifted her right hand and stretched it forth. The Drakka sniffed again, then its eyes hardened, the intelligence replaced by fury, and it snarled and tried to snap its jaws onto her flesh. Her feet tangled up as she tried to move, and she fell hard on her backside, her eyes wide with terror. The Drakka flexed its massive muscles, stretching the chains taut. A flash of blue light illuminated the chamber, temporarily blinding her. The Drakka shrieked in pain and anger.

Kai blinked rapidly until her vision cleared. Liu stood over her and offered his hand. She grabbed it, and he pulled her onto her feet.

"What were you doing?" he asked quietly, shifting his eyes from her to the other Chosen.

"I... I don't know."

"Never do that again."

Kai nodded. Her throat constricted, and swallowing didn't help. She retreated back to where the other Chosen stood and stared at the Drakka. There was something... familiar about the creature. She knew that was impossible, and yet she'd felt it. An intangible sensation deep down in her being.

What could it mean?

CHAPTER 5

The rest of their time with the Drakka was uneventful. Kai wanted to clear her mind, and Siran didn't feel like joining her, and so Liu followed her at a distance as she wandered the garden. The cobblestones were still slick from the rain, but the sun was high overhead and here and there she spotted sections of the pathway that were drying.

She couldn't get the sight of the Drakka from her mind. Glancing over her shoulder at Liu, she nodded for him to join her.

"Is everything all right?"

"Yes," she replied. "How much longer before the dragons arrive for the ceremony?"

"They should arrive within the next day or two. The storm delayed their arrival. While it isn't ideal, the servants are glad. It gives them more time to prepare for the ceremony. Everything was ruined from the rain."

One person's misfortune is another's blessing, she thought to herself. She closed her eyes as a wave of pain washed over her, but it quickly faded. The headaches had lessened over the past few days, and she hadn't needed to take any of the medicine the healer had given her.

"I want to ask you something."

"Speak your mind."

"I fear you will think I am crazy," Kai admitted.

"Fear should not stop you from seeking answers."

"How easily you say that." She stared at some flowers, trying to figure out how to phrase her question. "You said Drakka are not intelligent, but how do we know that?"

"We have studied them long enough to make that judgement based on their behavior. There are countless reasons why we believe this to be true. They are driven only by instinct. There are no leaders among their ranks. They consume everything without thought or concern for even their own continuation."

"Then why haven't we defeated them?"

Liu laughed, but there was nothing humorous about her question. "You are not the first to ask that, but I do not have an answer. Despite how many we kill, their numbers never seem to decrease."

Kai frowned, troubled by his words. She couldn't rid herself of the feeling that there was more to the Drakka than met the eye, that there was a depth to them that had yet to be understood. A gust of wind blew through the garden, and the scent of damp earth reminded her of home.

"Are my parents well? From the storm, I mean."

"They are fine. I confirmed so myself after the storm passed."

"That is good. Thank you for checking on them."

As they strolled along a path lined with vibrant camellia, Kai gathered her courage to voice her true question. "What if we've been wrong about the Drakka all this time?"

"How so?"

"What if they're smarter than we realize? Perhaps they've only led us to believe they lack intelligence."

"The notion that the Drakka could possess a level of intelligence we have yet to comprehend is unsettling, to say the least. But the empire's best minds have studied them extensively. Even if they are smarter than we know, we have strategies in place to protect ourselves."

"But what if our strategies are based on faulty assumptions?" Kai pressed on, her mind racing with the implications of her own words. "What if we need to rethink everything we know about the Drakka in order to truly defeat them?"

Liu regarded her thoughtfully. "I must admit that your questions give me pause, but not because I think you are crazy," he added, silencing her before she could protest. "Your line of thinking challenges everything we know, so it is difficult because... I do not have the answers. Let us assume you are correct about this. What then shall we do?"

Kai stared at him, speechless. What indeed? "Like you, I do not have an answer. Earlier..." she trailed off, uncertain if she should say anything.

"Earlier...?"

"I had the feeling *it* was familiar to me somehow."

"Have you encountered this one before?"

"No. Until today, I've never seen a Drakka. I know it doesn't make sense, but I *felt* it."

"I still do not think you are crazy, but I am concerned about this. I will speak with Master

Satoshi. Perhaps he can give us guidance. Did your dragon also feel it?"

Kai's eyes darted away from Liu. She couldn't tell him the truth. If the news broke that a Chosen could not hear the voice of their dragon, there was no telling what the response would be. People might accuse her mother of lying about feeling the Sign. She imagined it would result in dishonor.

"I've not consulted my dragon about this," Kai answered. It wasn't a lie, not really.

"I would suggest you do so. If your dragon felt it... well, we would need to investigate this further."

Kai nodded.

"In the meantime, do not speak of this to anyone else." Liu cleared his throat and changed the subject. "The ceremony is almost upon us. I imagine you are excited to meet your dragon face to face?"

"If I am honest, I am nervous. Being Chosen is a great honor, but I do not feel worthy."

"If you were not, your dragon would not have selected you. Still, I understand in my own way. I do not feel worthy of protecting a Chosen."

"Why not?"

Liu smiled. "You do not want to know of my faults."

"We are all flawed. You know that I am nervous and afraid. Tell me why you think you are not worthy."

"Your life is in my hands," he replied. "I am not confident that I am capable of ensuring your safety. It is an immense burden."

"I know I've only been here for a few days, but there doesn't seem to be any danger here. I think things will be fine. Besides, once I am Sworn, you will no longer be assigned to me."

A horn sounded in the distance. Kai startled, her heart leaping in her chest. Liu turned his attention west.

"They're early," he said.

"Who?"

"The dragons."

CHAPTER 6

The courtyard was a cacophony of voices as people gathered to watch the arrival of the dragons. Liu and Kai stood among the crowd, starting westward. The silhouettes of a dozen dragons appeared on the horizon, their majestic forms cutting through the sky with grace and power.

The people around her gasped and whispered in awe. Kai held her breath as she watched the dragons draw nearer, their scales shimmering in the sunlight. Each dragon was unique, with vibrant colors and patterns that set them apart from one another. Emerald, sapphire, amethyst and other colors greeted them, but Kai's attention was drawn to one dragon in particular. Its scales glistened like polished gray hematite, and Kai had no doubt that was her dragon.

The buzzing in Kai's ears intensified, building to a crescendo and drowning out the sounds of the crowd around her. Thankfully, there was no pain, but that didn't make her feel any better. The dragons landed in the field outside of the castle, each one issuing a thunderous roar which she faintly heard. The noise was overwhelming, and she felt her legs grow weak. Fearing she was about to pass out, she grabbed hold of Liu's arm. The buzzing abruptly stopped.

"Another headache?" he asked lowly.

Kai offered a brief nod, not wanting to add to his concerns. "It passed quickly," she replied.

A cheer erupted from the crowd as a figure strode across the ramparts of the wall. He raised his right hand, calling for silence.

"Good people of Ikje, thank you for coming to honor our Chosen. This group is only a dozen strong, but as we all know, the strength of a rider is worth many. Tonight, we will celebrate our Chosen with a feast, and tomorrow, they will be Sworn!"

The crowd bellowed their approval, and the man on the parapet returned to the castle.

"Who was that?" Kai asked.

"That was Master Satoshi."

As the sun began to set, lanterns and braziers were lit around the courtyard, bathing everything in a warm light. Long tables were arranged in the courtyard, laden with an abundance of food and drink, and soon, the courtyard was alive with laughter and chatter as people mingled, celebrating the upcoming ceremony. Kai sat between Siran and Ichiro, swept up in the festivities, her earlier doubts and worries momentarily pushed aside by the joyous atmosphere. She ate and drank with the others, listening to stories of past ceremonies and legendary deeds of riders from their history.

As the night progressed, the crowd slowly dispersed and a chill settled in the air. Kai excused herself from the table and slipped away into the shadows of the courtyard, making her way through the maze-like corridors of the castle. She found a secluded alcove overlooking the moonlit landscape beyond the walls and leaned against the cool stone, wrapping her arms around herself as a shiver ran down her spine.

The moon was full and bright, casting a silvery glow over the landscape. From this vantage point, she could see the dragons resting in the field beyond the walls, their forms barely visible in the darkness.

"Kai?"

She started at the sound of her name and turned to see Liu, his expression unreadable.

"Are you all right?"

"Yes. Just... thinking."

"Master Satoshi has requested your presence."

"Is it about what I told you?"

He nodded in reply. Kai was exhausted and wanted nothing more than to crawl into her bed, but she knew Master Satoshi's request was an order, not an invitation. She pushed off the wall and Liu escorted her through the hall.

"What did he say when you told him?"

"Not much. He listened, and then asked to see you. I suppose he wants more details."

Kai followed Liu in silence. They climbed a circular staircase to the highest tower of the castle and paused outside a set of oak doors. Liu gave a firm knock, announcing their presence, and they were bid to enter.

Kai entered the room first. Master Satoshi sat at a large wooden desk cluttered with scrolls and other parchments. He looked up and motioned for her to take a seat. The room was brightly lit by a myriad of lanterns. She walked to his desk and sat down, folding her hands in her lap.

Master Satoshi's face was chiseled with sharp, angular features—high cheekbones, a strong jawline, and a straight, narrow nose that looked as though it could have been sculpted from stone. Dark, penetrating eyes reflected the calm of a seasoned warrior, and his jet-black hair was tied back in a soldier's knot. He exuded a quiet confidence, his presence commanding respect and attention. Awestruck, Kai stared at him in silence. The man was a hero, a paragon of strength and honor.

"Liu tells me you felt a connection to the Drakka. I would like to hear you recount the experience in your own words."

"Yes, my lord." Kai ran her fingers along the material of her clothes, looking for a seam to run under her nails, but there wasn't one. "It was earlier, when we were studying the creature. Liu had asked me to come closer to it, and when it looked at me..."

"Go on."

"I felt something. It's hard to describe, but it was as though I knew this creature."

"Liu said you've never seen a Drakka before today. Is that correct?"

"Yes, my lord."

Satoshi's eyebrows furrowed in thought. "And what has your dragon said about this matter?"

"I have not spoken to it yet."

Satoshi's eyes moved from her to Liu, who was standing at attention near the door. "Leave us," he instructed. Liu did as commanded and closed the door behind him.

"Is there anything else you want me to know?"

"Not that I can think of," Kai replied.

Satoshi sat back in his chair and stared at her, his gaze holding the intensity of an unyielding tempest. "Trust is a two-way path, Kai Lin. How can I trust you if you lie to my face?"

Kai's cheeks flushed with warmth. "I-I'm sorry, my lord." Her hands trembled as she fidgeted. Satoshi's expression softened slightly as he observed her distress.

"Honesty is paramount in our order. We rely on trust and transparency to uphold our values and traditions," he explained with a measured tone. "Now, let us try this again. Is there anything else you want me to know?"

Kai's eyes watered with tears, and despite her best efforts to hold them in, one slipped free and slid down her cheek. She opened her mouth to speak, closed it, and clenched her fists. What she was about to say could bring disaster upon her family.

"I have never spoken to my dragon."

CHAPTER 7

"I suspected as much."

Kai waited for the confusion, the outrage, the repercussions that would surely follow. Instead, Master Satoshi remained eerily calm, his gaze unwavering. Kai's heart pounded in her chest, unsure of what would come next.

"Why have you not spoken to your dragon?"

"I... I cannot hear it. There is only a buzzing sound in my mind. I've tried countless times to communicate with it, but it is no use. I fear I am not truly Chosen."

"Silence does not mean absence. It could be that your dragon is waiting for you to listen in a different way."

Confusion clouded Kai's mind. What did he mean by a different way? She had been trying to communicate with her dragon through thoughts and feelings as she had been taught, but to no avail.

"I have tried everything I can think of," she said.

"You need not fear judgment here. I am not quick to condemn, especially in matters concerning the bond. It is a sacred connection, one that cannot be forced or coerced. For some, the bond is tentative, weak. It is like a muscle. It needs to be used, exercised. You are not the first Chosen to have this problem, though it is not common."

Kai felt a weight lift off her shoulders at his words. She met his gaze, seeing understanding and empathy reflected in his eyes. "I was afraid..."

"You were afraid of being misunderstood," he finished for her. "But I assure you, I have seen many riders face similar struggles when it comes to communicating with their dragons. It is a process that takes time and patience. For many, it is merely a matter of meeting their dragon. Seeing them in the flesh can help solidify the bond."

Kai absorbed Master Satoshi's words, feeling a glimmer of hope ignite within her. His words eased the fears that had plagued her for so long. Perhaps he was right. She nodded slowly, grateful for his understanding and guidance. The words of the healer suddenly came to her.

"Someone told me I had a strange energy in my *ki*. Do you know what she meant?"

"*Ki* is the life force that flows within us, connecting us to all things in the world. It is said that each individual's *ki* is unique, a reflection of their essence and spirit. I am no healer, but I would wager a guess that the shame you feel has muddied your *ki*. Cleanse it, and it may help to unlock your connection to your dragon."

"How would I do that? Even with your explanation, I'm not entirely sure what my *ki* is."

"The easiest way is to meditate. Visualize your *ki* and filter out the negative energy that taints it. The process is time consuming, but I believe you will find it well worth the effort."

"Thank you, my lord. You have lifted a great burden from me."

"I only do what I would expect anyone else to do for me. Go and get some rest. The ceremony is tomorrow, and you will need a clear mind."

Kai rose from her chair and offered a bow to Satoshi. He hid his smile by yawning and waved her away. When she reached the door, he told her to inform Liu he was dismissed for the evening. She nodded and stepped into the hall. Liu was leaning against the wall, his arms folded across his chest and his eyes half lidded. At the sound of the creaking door, he straightened.

"He said you are dismissed, which appears to be a good thing since you were dozing off just now."

"I was merely resting my eyes," Liu replied.

A faint smile graced Kai's lips, the first genuine one she had shown in quite some time.

"How did it go?"

"Much better than I expected," she said. "Master Satoshi is as gracious as he is wise."

"Good. What did he say about your Drakka experience?"

"Nothing. I think he's as baffled about it as I am."

"Why did he keep you so long?"

"We talked about other things," Kai replied evasively. "He suggested I cleanse my *ki*."

Liu grunted in response. They returned to the main floor of the castle, and Liu walked with her until they reached the door to her room.

"Get some sleep," he said as he departed. "Tomorrow will be a long day."

Kai opened the door and slipped inside. The other Chosen were in bed, and judging by the chorus of snores and heavy breathing, they were all sleeping. She quietly crept to her bed and stripped down to her undergarments, then laid down and stared up at the shadows that shrouded the ceiling. For the first time in years, she felt at peace.

Satoshi's words echoed in her mind, urging her to cleanse her *ki* to make way for a stronger connection with her dragon. Closing her eyes, Kai focused on her breathing. She delved deep into herself, visualizing her *ki* as a bright orb within her core. Surrounding it was a murky haze that dulled its radiance.

With each breath, she imagined the light growing stronger, pushing back against the darkness that sought to dim it. The weight of shame and self-doubt began to lift as she focused on letting go of the negative energy that had clouded her spirit. It was a slow process, requiring patience and fortitude, but Kai was determined to forge a deeper connection with her dragon.

The haze dissipated, and a faint whisper tickled at the edges of her consciousness. It was not a sound she heard with her ears but a sensation that resonated within her being. Intrigued, Kai opened herself to it, inviting the whisper into herself.

Images flickered in her mind's eye—vivid flashes of scales, an endless expanse of azure sky, and the sensation of soaring through clouds. The whisper grew stronger, manifesting as a gentle warmth spreading from her core. In that moment of surrender, Kai felt a presence, a gentle touch brushing against her spirit.

The buzzing she had always heard began to shift, morphing into a symphony of harmonious vibrations that resonated deep within her soul. It was a feeling that transcended words. Like a gentle breeze stirring dormant embers, she felt a presence rousing within her. It was as if a part of herself she had long neglected was awakening, stretching its wings in the darkness of her inner self. The connection she had yearned for but thought unattainable was now tangible, a thread linking her to a being of immense power and ancient wisdom.

Tears pricked at the corners of Kai's eyes as she reveled in the newfound connection. It was as if a missing piece of her soul had finally been found, completing a puzzle she hadn't even known was incomplete.

Exhaustion overtook her, and as she drifted off to sleep, she was comforted by the knowledge that she was no longer alone.

CHAPTER 8

When Kai opened her eyes, the warm light of the morning sun streamed in through the window. She sat up and stretched, a newfound energy coursing through her body. For the first time in her life, she was eager to meet her dragon in person.

She reached out with her thoughts, but although she sensed the same strong presence from the previous night, she still couldn't hear her dragon's voice. Satoshi's words lingered in her mind, and she was confident that today would be the day she finally heard her dragon speak.

Kai climbed out of bed and noticed a pile of clothes folded neatly atop the chest at the end of her bed. A pair of black leather boots sat beside the clothes, and they shined with fresh polish.

"They expect us to look nice," Siran said. "The Ceremony of Oaths is sacred, so on and so forth." Kai looked at her. She was fully dressed in the same clothes but was lying in her bed, propped up on her elbows. Suddenly feeling immodest, she hurriedly dressed herself.

"You don't think it's important?"

"Of course I do, but after we are trained, they throw us against the Drakka. Who cares what we wear to the ceremony? No one is going to remember that. What they remember is how we die."

"That's a little depressing, don't you think?"

"It is, but that doesn't make it any less true. Besides, it's not like anyone will be able to see these under the armor."

Siran's dark words couldn't bring her spirits down. The joy inside her was too strong to be quenched.

"That's fair," Kai replied. She'd almost forgotten that she'd been fitted for armor before leaving home. She ran her hands along the bright red material of her new clothes, admiring the softness.

"Silk," Siran said, as if reading her thoughts.

Kai nodded, impressed by the fine quality of the fabric. It felt like a caress against her skin, a feeling she wasn't accustomed to. As she finished putting her boots on, the door creaked open, and Liu entered the room with the other guards. His expression softened as he took in Kai's appearance.

"You look nice," he said, a hint of pride in his voice.

Kai felt her cheeks warm at the unexpected compliment. "Thank you."

"We've got several things to do before the ceremony, so we should get to it."

"Can we eat first? I'm hungry."

"Breakfast is being served now. Just be sure not to get your clothes dirty."

Kai and the other Chosen went to the dining hall and ate a quick meal, then they were ushered to the armory. Inside, the air was thick with the scent of metal and leather. Rows of weapons lined the walls, each gleaming under the warm glow of oil lamps. Kai marveled at the craftsmanship on display, from the intricate engravings that adorned the blades of swords to the finely woven strings that dangled from their hilts.

A white-haired smith approached them, his weathered face breaking into a toothy grin. "Honored Chosen," he greeted, gesturing for them to follow him to a row of armor stands, each holding a set of gleaming armor.

"Let's start with you," he said, pointing at Jiro.

"Lucky," Ichiro muttered, playfully punching his brother in the arm.

Jiro stepped forward and the smith took a few measurements, then motioned to one of the stands. "This one is yours." Kai watched as the smith aided with putting the individual pieces on, adjusting straps and buckles with practiced ease. Jiro stood tall in his new armor, the metal plates clinking together as he moved. Next, it was Ichiro's turn. Despite his playful demeanor, Kai could sense there was a fire within him that burned fiercely. Commoner or not, something told her that he would be a great warrior.

Once Ichiro was suited up, it was Siran's turn. She stood confidently as the smith worked around her, his hands deftly securing each piece in place. Siran looked every bit the warrior, and Kai was glad to count her as a friend.

Finally, it was Kai's turn. She stepped forward eagerly, her heart pounding in anticipation. The smith measured her, then pointed at the stand that held her armor. As he helped her don the pieces, Kai felt a sense of belonging wash over her. The weight of the armor was comforting rather than burdensome, and it fit her perfectly.

Once fully armored, Kai took a few experimental steps, testing the flexibility. Surprisingly, she found it easier to move in than she had anticipated, the armor fitting her like a second skin. She flexed her fingers within the cotton gloves and smiled in admiration.

After each of them had been outfitted, the white-haired smith nodded in approval, a glint of pride in his eyes. "You all wear it well," he said. "It is an honor to have crafted your armor. Now, you must choose a weapon."

The room was filled with an array of options, all of them deadly. The Chosen spread out, and Kai walked over to a rack of swords. Her hands ghosted over the polished handles of a few, but nothing caught her eye. She continued to the far wall and her eyes fell upon a sword unlike any other in the room.

The blade was as dark as the void and sharp enough to split a hair. Its edge, honed to perfection, caught the light in razor-thin, iridescent lines that seemed to dance before her eyes. The surface, smooth as a still lake at midnight, bore intricate runes that emanated magical power. The hilt was wrought from lustrous ebony and wrapped in dark leather. The crossguard flared out like the wings of a raven, its tips fashioned into menacing, curved talons, providing balance and protection. Nestled in the pommel was a perfect, unblemished obsidian, its surface as dark and reflective as a night sky without stars.

Kai reached out and wrapped her fingers around the hilt, pulling it off the wall prongs. Something clattered to the floor, and she whirled around in surprise. The smith's eyes were wide, and he dropped to his knees and pressed his forehead to the floor. Kai looked at Liu, who was staring at her in a similar fashion.

"I'm sorry," she said. "Should I not have touched it? I'll return it."

She turned to put the sword back, but the smith's words stopped her.

"That blade has not been touched since its creation. It was forged from volcanic rock, and the smith who crafted it weaved a spell into the metal. Only one baptized in the blood of dragons can wield it."

Kai's eyes roamed the length of the blade, then she looked at the smith, her brows scrunched in confusion. "I have never seen a dragon, let alone touched the blood of one."

The smith and Liu engaged in a whispered conversation, then Liu rushed out of the room, leaving Kai further bewildered. The smith approached her slowly, almost reverently.

"Whether you know it or not, you must have come in contact with dragon blood. There is no way you would be able to touch the sword otherwise. Unless…"

"Unless what?" she asked.

"Unless the spell has faded. I am too old now to risk the pain it would cause." The smith turned to the other Chosen. "Would one of you be willing to try holding the sword?"

They stared at Kai as though she were some sort of apparition, all except Siran. The woman confidently strode over and extended her right hand. Kai offered her the weapon, and as soon as Siran touched it, a dazzling burst of energy shocked her. Siran cried out and staggered back, pressing her hand to her chest.

"I am sorry, but I needed to be sure," the smith said. "Go and see the healers. They will tend to your hand and ensure you are fit for the ceremony."

Siran departed, and Kai couldn't help but feel a twinge of guilt even though it wasn't her fault. "I do not want this sword," she said softly.

"It was made for you," the smith insisted. "What happened to her has happened to all who have tried to touch that blade. The fact you hold it now and are not immobilized with pain confirms you are its owner now."

His words weighed heavily on her as she gazed at the weapon, torn between the allure of the weapon and the danger it seemed to pose. She stilled her racing heart and reached out to her dragon. Again, she did not hear a voice, but something told her she should keep it. After a moment of contemplation, she nodded.

"I will take it."

The smith smiled broadly. "A wise choice. I am sure you will wield it with honor and strength. It is a weapon meant for one destined for greatness."

CHAPTER 9

Once Liu returned, he ordered the Chosen back to their room. As they made their way through the hall, the weight of the sword in its sheath at Kai's side felt both daunting and exhilarating. She couldn't help but steal glances at the weapon, all while the words of the white-haired smith echoed in her mind.

Back in their chambers, Kai stood by her bed, watching the other Chosen as they sat together, whispering and occasionally looking in her direction. She huffed loudly, and when Jiro looked at her, she met his gaze.

"If you are going to talk ill of me, do it to my face and not like cowards." The words poured from her unbidden, and she was surprised at herself.

"We are talking about you, but not badly," Jiro replied. "We're discussing what is written about the Blooded One. I think you are the one the scrolls speak of."

"Blooded One?" Kai asked. "Is this about the dragon blood? I told that man I've never seen or touched a dragon!"

"Calm down," Jiro soothed. "It's a good thing if you're this person."

"Not really," another of the Chosen said. It was a boy named Kazu. "The writings could mean she is evil."

Kai scowled. "What are you talking about? I'm not evil, and I'm not whatever the Blooded One is."

"You don't know what the Blooded One is?" Jiro asked. "Everyone knows."

"She wouldn't know because she's not like us," Kazu said. "She's a noble."

Jiro broke away from the group and came to stand beside Kai. "You really don't know what is written?"

"No."

"Can I tell you?"

Kai shrugged. "Sure."

"It's not exactly a prophecy, but it kind of is. It says that someone who has been bathed in a dragon's blood will save the empire."

"*Tsk*, that's not what it says." They both turned to see Siran. She was holding her hand close to her chest.

"Are you all right?" Kai asked. "I'm so sorry."

"It wasn't your fault. It's not like you made the sword hurt me... did you?"

"Of course not!"

Siran smirked. "I know. It was a joke. My hand is fine. The pain was intense, but the healers put some sort of balm on it and it feels normal now."

"I'm glad you're not hurt," Kai said.

"Me too. Why are you letting Jiro fill your head with nonsense?"

"It's not nonsense," Jiro protested.

"Some might argue otherwise. Either way, the scrolls do not say the Blooded One will save the empire. And the scrolls don't use the term Blooded One. That's something zealots came up with."

"Everyone uses it," Jiro said defensively.

"I'm not judging you," Siran replied. "I'm just saying."

"I've never heard of this prophecy or whatever," Kai said. "What is it?"

"I'm not surprised. Commoners latch onto it because they think this mythical person is going to lift them out of poverty or something. As nobles, we don't put our faith in fables."

Jiro glowered at Siran but said nothing.

"It's a poem of sorts," Siran continued. "I remember it because my grandmother used to recite it to me. How does it start again... Oh, that's right.

When the blood of a dragon stains the pure,
A child shall rise to endure.
With flames that dance and shadows that sprawl,
This harbinger shall heed destiny's call.
Upon their ascent, the world shall see,
A dawn of hope or a night of misery.
For in the heart of the dragon's kin,
Lies the power to save or sin."

Kai digested the words as best as she could, but it didn't make any sense to her. "I don't see the connection," she said.

"Of course not. You have common sense, which isn't so common with them," Siran nodded her head toward the others. "You'd think it would be. I mean, it's in the title commoner." She scoffed.

Kai smiled. She didn't agree with Siran putting people down, but she did find that last bit humorous.

"We're not stupid because we believe in something different than you," Jiro said. "Some of us have put our hope into something higher than ourselves."

Before Siran could respond, the door to their chamber swung open and Liu strode in with the other guards.

"Drakka have been spotted in the woods," he announced. "Master Satoshi feels it is best to hold the ceremony now and then send you all to Dangju for training. Take a moment to pack to your things, then meet us in the courtyard."

Kai felt some relief when the guards left. Liu hadn't mentioned her sword or the strange prophecy, which meant he probably didn't believe in it any more than she did. She focused on the urgency of the moment and opened the chest at the end of her bed, gathering her belongings. The other Chosen rushed about frantically, their voices a chorus of concern.

Once everyone was prepared, they exited the room and made their way to the courtyard. An announcement must have been made because there was a large crowd already gathered. The air was tense with anticipation, and Kai's stomach churned at the realization that life as she knew it was about to change forever.

A short rectangular platform had been erected in the center of the courtyard, and Master Satoshi was there waiting for them.

The Chosen filed onto the platform and lined up in an orderly row, facing the crowd. Kai looked for her parents and spotted them to her left. They didn't wave, but she could tell by their expressions they were proud of her.

Master Satoshi raised his hand for silence, and the buzz of the crowd gradually hushed. His voice carried through the courtyard with authority, each word echoing off the stone walls.

"The Ceremony of Oaths is a sacred ceremony, created by our ancestors to honor the bond between dragon and rider. A person is not Chosen based on birthright or merit, but by destiny. These men and women stand before you as a symbol of hope and strength, chosen by their dragons to protect our empire from the encroaching darkness."

He paused and looked down the line of Chosen, his gaze lingering on Kai who stood at the end of the line. She felt his stare and looked at him, meeting his eyes briefly before he turned his attention back to the crowd.

"For centuries, we have lived under the threat of the Drakka, but every day, hope blossoms. Every new Chosen is a promise for an end to our plight. They fight—we *all* fight—to bring an end to the Drakka."

Kai could feel the weight of Master Satoshi's words pressing down on her, the gravity of their calling settling deep in her bones. She glanced at the others standing beside her. Their faces were a mixture of determination and fear. They were all so young to be burdened with such responsibility, one far greater than themselves.

"Let us remember the sacrifices made by those who came before us and honor their legacy with our actions," Master Satoshi continued. "The strength of our empire lies not in the grandeur of our cities, but in the courage and unity of its people."

The courtyard fell into a solemn silence. Kai's heart thundered in her chest. This was it. She was finally going to meet her dragon. It had long been a day she dreaded, but now her soul longed for it.

"Let us begin the Ceremony of Oaths."

CHAPTER 10

The sound of beating wings echoed through the air as the dragons that had arrived the night before soared over the walls, landing behind the platform. They were a magnificent sight, their scales shimmering in the sunlight. They were much larger than Kai expected, even after glimpsing them previously. She could feel the power emanating from them, a primal force that made her heart race with fear and excitement.

Her emotions were mirrored by the crowd, who murmured among themselves. The dragons trumpeted their presence, and Kai could feel her clothes vibrating from the sound. As one, the Chosen fell onto their knees and bowed their heads, paying homage to their more powerful counterparts.

"Siran," Master Satoshi called out. "Rise and approach your dragon."

Siran stood, her steps confident as she walked towards the dragon that awaited her. The dragon was a regal creature with scales as red as rubies, contrasting sharply against the dark colors of the stone wall behind it. She stopped a few feet short, and the dragon leaned down, putting its face inches from Siran's.

Master Satoshi joined them, holding a golden bowl and a dagger. Siran held her hand out, and Master Satoshi ran the blade across her palm. Kai admired Siran for not making a sound or flinching. The red dragon raised its front left leg and Master Satoshi gently lifted one of its scales, cutting the leathery skin underneath. He collected drops of blood from them both into the bowl, then stirred it with the dagger.

Kai waited expectantly, but nothing happened. Master Satoshi carried the bowl to a brazier and poured the blood into it. The flames roared upward, changing briefly to the same color as the dragon's scales, then returned to normal. Master Satoshi walked back to Siran's side.

"Speak the vows," he said.

Siran straightened and spoke loudly for all to hear. "By the sacred flame and the ancient bond we share, I vow to uphold the honor of our ancestors, to protect our lands and its people with courage and wisdom. With my dragon as my guide and my strength, I pledge my life to the guardianship of our realm, now and for all eternity."

The dragon lifted its head and turned its attention to Master Satoshi. Projecting its thoughts, it spoke to everyone who was present. *By the breath of fire and the skies we soar, I vow to honor our ancient bond, to protect our lands and its creatures with might and grace. With my rider as my heart and my spirit, I pledge my life to the guardianship of our realm, now and for all eternity.*

Then together, Siran and her dragon said, "As one soul in two bodies, we vow to stand as guardians of our world. In unity, strength, and unwavering loyalty, for the light of our bond shall guide us, now and forevermore."

Kai was in awe. The dragon's voice was deep and gruff, unlike anything she imagined. Was her dragon's voice the same?

"You are all witness to the Oaths," Master Satoshi said. "Let no one question their devotion to the empire, nor to one another. Now they will take to the sky for their first flight."

The red dragon lowered itself to the ground, and Siran used the ridges of his scales to climb up his shoulder, settling herself between his shoulder blades. There was no saddle, no straps, nothing at all to keep her from falling off the dragon's back. Kai frowned, wondering how she would stay put. Siran leaned forward, practically lying down, and grabbed hold of the scales on the dragon's neck.

With a mighty leap, the beast was in the air, his massive wings stirring up dirt in the courtyard, carrying them upward. Kai watched in awe as Siran and her dragon soared together, their figures becoming smaller against the vast expanse of the sky. The crowd erupted into cheers, their voices carrying up to the heavens.

As she gazed up at them, a mix of emotions swirled within Kai. There was a pang of envy at the strength of Siran's bond with her dragon, and an underlying fear of the unknown that lay ahead. Would she and her dragon be as majestic together? Would they form a connection as strong and unbreakable? Her eyes slowly moved from the sky to the gray dragon.

Can you hear me? she asked, trying to project her voice through their bond.

Silence met her question, and if the dragon could hear her, it gave no physical indication.

She considered what Master Satoshi told her and forced her doubts away. Once they completed the Oaths, she was confident their bond would strengthen enough to communicate with one another.

Eventually the red dragon came back into view, circling above the crowd before landing in his original spot. Siran leaped down to the ground, her face flushed with pride and exhilaration. Master Satoshi nodded at her, a smile tugging at the corners of his lips.

"There are few things that compare to flying with your dragon," he said. "We are honored to witness your Oaths. Siran Himura, you are no longer Chosen. You are now Sworn."

The crowd roared with excitement once more, and Kai felt a sudden urge to cry. She finally understood the significance of the Ceremony of Oaths. Even though rider and dragon were already bonded, there was something incredibly emotional about the ritual itself. She managed to hold back the tears, and as Siran returned to her place among the Chosen, Kai smiled at her.

"Ichiro," Master Satoshi said. "Rise and approach your dragon."

Ichiro did as commanded, striding across the platform and onto the cobbled stones to stand before an enormous blue dragon whose scales glittered like sapphires. Its eyes locked onto Ichiro, and a sense of recognition passed between them. Without hesitation, Ichiro reached out his hand, palm open, and the dragon leaned down to nuzzle his fingertips gently. It was a moment of pure connection, a silent understanding that needed no words.

Master Satoshi stepped forward with the golden bowl and dagger once more, cleaned and ready. With practiced ease, he cut their flesh and drew blood, mixing it in the bowl before igniting it in the brazier. The flames danced in a mesmerizing display before settling into a steady glow. Ichiro and his dragon stood face to face as they recited their vows, their voices intertwining in a harmonious echo that resonated through the courtyard.

As they finished, the blue dragon dipped its head in a solemn bow, and Ichiro placed his hand on its massive snout, rubbing the scales.

"You are all witness to the Oaths," Master Satoshi repeated. "Let no one question their devotion to the empire, nor to one another. Now they will take to the sky for their first flight."

The blue dragon knelt before Ichiro, and he clambered onto its back. With a powerful thrust of its wings, the dragon launched itself into the air, carrying Ichiro aloft. The crowd watched in hushed awe as they circled above just as Siran and her dragon had done moments before.

The ceremony continued in the same fashion, with Jiro going after his brother. He was bonded to a green dragon whose scales were like polished jade. Next was Kazu, followed by Reika. Kai watched each ritual with a mix of reverence and excitement. Eleven Chosen were now Sworn, and Kai was the only who one remained.

It was finally her turn.

"Kai, rise and approach your dragon."

Kai felt her heart leap into her throat as all eyes turned to her. The importance of the moment settled upon her shoulders, and for a brief instant, doubt gnawed at the edges of her resolve. She took a deep breath and walked towards the great gray dragon, her steps faltering slightly in her nervousness. The dragon regarded her with eyes that seemed to pierce through her very soul, assessing her with a gaze that was both intimidating and strangely comforting.

Master Satoshi joined them, his presence reassuring as he performed the ritual of the blood. Kai gritted her teeth against the pain of the cut on her palm, willing herself to remain stoic like Siran had. The dragon watched intently, a rumble reverberating in its chest. Master Satoshi collected its blood next, and the golden bowl shimmered in the sunlight as he approached the brazier.

With a steady hand, he poured the blood into the flames. The fire erupted in a dazzling display of silver light, flickering and dancing with an ethereal glow. Kai felt a surge of energy course through her, a tingling sensation that pulled at the edges of her *ki*. Her dragon was a male. She wasn't sure how she knew that. She just... knew.

"Speak the vows," Master Satoshi instructed.

She stared at the dragon, the words suddenly fleeing her memory. She'd learned the vow when she was young, had repeated it countless times in her short life. Why now, at the most important moment of her life, did the words elude her grasp? Master Satoshi cleared his throat, drawing her attention. His stern gaze jolted something within her, and the words came rushing back. She drew a steadying breath.

"By the sacred flame and the ancient bond we share, I vow to uphold the honor of our ancestors, to protect our lands and its people with courage and wisdom. With my dragon as my guide and my strength, I pledge my life to the guardianship of our realm, now and for all eternity."

The dragon regarded her for a moment before leaning closer. He sniffed the air around her, his warm breath washing over her face. Kai could feel the weight of his presence and it sent a chill down her spine. Lifting his head, he projected his voice for everyone to hear.

This is not my rider.

CHAPTER 11

Kai's heart plummeted at the dragon's words, and a cold dread settled in the pit of her stomach. The revelation hung heavy in the air, stirring a wave of murmurs and gasps through the crowd. Kai's pulse pounded in her ears, her mind struggling to comprehend the dragon's words.

"This cannot be," Master Satoshi declared, his voice carrying his authority despite a flicker of uncertainty in his eyes. "The bond is predetermined by the ancient rites. There can be no mistake."

The dragon huffed, puffs of smoke escaping its nostrils as it regarded Kai with an intensity that made her feel exposed, vulnerable. She sensed a ripple of unease pass through the Sworn behind her, their whispers blending into a dissonant hum that resonated in her bones. She stole a glance at Master

Satoshi, searching for some sign of reassurance or explanation in his expression, but his features remained stoic and unreadable.

"I am Kai Lin," she said, her words sounding feeble even to her own ears. "Daughter of Ryoko Lin and Sho Lin. My mother received the Sign when I was in her womb. I *am* your rider."

You are not.

Before anyone could speak further, a figure emerged from the outskirts of the courtyard. Clad in dark robes that billowed around them like shadows given form, the newcomer strode purposefully towards the platform where Kai and the dragon were. A hood obscured their features, casting a veil of mystery over their identity as they drew closer, but Kai caught a glimpse of glacial blue eyes. The stranger's presence exuded an otherworldly aura, a sense of power that commanded attention.

As the stranger reached the foot of the platform, they raised a hand and pushed back their hood, revealing a face that was both familiar and foreign to Kai. It was a face she had seen countless times in the mirror... her own.

Confusion and disbelief warred within Kai as she tried to make sense of what she saw. Was this a dark spirit disguising itself as her? Or had she fallen under some sort of curse? The woman, who appeared to be her but also not quite, extended her hand towards the gray dragon. He nuzzled his snout against her affectionately.

The woman's eyes swept over the gathering, landing on Master Satoshi. "The bond between dragon and rider is not always as straightforward as tradition dictates."

"Who are you to interrupt the sacred ceremony?"

A ghost of a smile pulled at the woman's lips. "I am Akuhara Lin, daughter of Ryoko Lin and Sho Lin, and I have come to claim my dragon."

A stunned silence settled over the courtyard. Master Satoshi's brows were scrunched in disbelief.

"Impossible," Kai whispered. A surge of conflicting emotions coursed through her—confusion, anger, and a deep-seated fear. How could this woman claim to share her bloodline and lineage? Was this some elaborate ruse, a deception woven with dark magic to disrupt the ritual? And yet the dragon himself said Kai was not his rider.

"Explain yourselves," Master Satoshi demanded, glancing from Akuhara to Kai.

She speaks true, the gray dragon rumbled. *Akuhara is my rider.*

Akuhara climbed onto the dragon's back, a smug expression on her face. Master Satoshi stood still, clearly confused. Finally, he looked at Kai, anger burning in his eyes.

"Did you lie about being Chosen?"

"No! I would never dishonor myself or my family."

"Take her to the dungeon," he commanded. "Her fate will be decided after the ceremony." He turned to Akuhara. "You must complete the Oaths."

Liu came to stand near Kai, and he grabbed onto her arm with a firm grip. She looked at him pleadingly, but he wouldn't look her in the eyes.

"There's no need," Akuhara replied. "I do not fight for the empire."

Master Satoshi sputtered. "Riders serve *only* the empire. If you do not fight for the empire, who do you fight for?"

Akuhara laughed briefly, then her expression turned serious. "I fight for the Drakka."

Horrified whispers erupted among the crowd of onlookers. Soldiers drew their swords, and Master Satoshi clenched his jaw. "Blasphemy!"

A horn blared, followed by the ringing of the bell tower. The silence of the courtyard turned into chaos as panic spread through the crowd like wildfire. The Sworn looked to Master Satoshi for guidance.

"You will all be witnesses," Akuhara shouted. "The empire will burn!"

With that, the gray dragon took to the sky. People scrambled in all directions, cries of fear and disbelief mingling with the ominous tolling of the bell tower. Kai found herself frozen in place, her mind reeling. Her parents would have the answers. They could explain to Master Satoshi that this was all a mistake. The Sworn would hunt down the doppelganger, and Kai would get her dragon back.

"Come with me," Liu said, guiding her through the turmoil toward the castle.

"My parents. They were in the crowd. They can—"

"That's the least of our worries right now. Didn't you hear the bell? We're under attack."

Kai looked over her shoulder, trying to spot her parents. They were nowhere in sight. She prayed they were safe and allowed herself to be led by Liu. Master Satoshi, trailed by the new Sworn, followed them inside the castle.

"Once the dragons are saddled, you will all flee to Dangju," he said. "I sent word to them days ago informing them of your arrival. You will train there, and report back here once you are done. Do not stop once you leave these walls. Go straight to Dangju."

"Yes, Master," they said in unison.

"As for you," he continued, looking at Kai, "I demand answers to your deception."

"I have deceived no one," she replied. "My parents are here. You can ask them, and they will tell you the same."

Master Satoshi looked at Liu. "Go find them."

Liu offered a quick bow and rushed off.

"Can we not stay and fight?" Siran asked. "I have trained with a sword most of my life. There is nothing anyone can teach me in Dangju."

"There is more to being a rider than wielding a blade," Master Satoshi answered. "You must learn about your bond and how to strengthen it. You will go to Dangju as I have commanded."

Siran lowered her head in submission, but Kai knew she was not happy. She was a warrior, and warriors did not run from battle.

Master Satoshi turned his attention back to Kai. His accusation hung over her like a dark cloud, but she had spoken the truth. She clenched her fists, fighting against the urge to lash out in frustration at the injustice of it all.

Liu returned with her parents in tow. Tears streamed down her mother's face, and her father was pale as though he were going to be ill.

"Kai's fate hangs by a thread," Master Satoshi said to them. "Speak honestly with me and she may yet be spared. Did you receive the Sign?"

Ryoko nodded. "I did."

"Describe it to me."

"At the Binding, I laid my hands on several eggs and felt nothing. When I touched the last one, warmth spread through my stomach, and I felt a kick. The Inquisitor who was present confirmed it."

"And you do not know this Akuhara?"

"I am... not sure."

"What do you mean?"

Ryoko choked back a sob. "I bore two children in my womb, but one was stillborn."

Master Satoshi frowned. "You had a first born that died upon birth?"

"No. I gave birth to twins."

CHAPTER 12

Kai felt as though she had been punched in the chest. Twins? Her mother had never mentioned anything about that.

"I'm sorry," Ryoko said, looking at her. "I should have told you."

"That doesn't answer my question," Master Satoshi growled. "What does a stillborn baby have to do with anything?"

"You saw the resemblance, as we all did," Sho answered. "She looked just like Kai. My wife thinks—*we* think it could be her."

Master Satoshi rubbed his hands over his face. "You said yourself the baby was stillborn. How could Akuhara be your child?"

"I know how it sounds, my lord, even to my own ears," Ryoko said. "And yet, she is a reflection of Kai. It is her. I know it."

"How do you know?"

"Mother's intuition."

"Was she left with a healer?" Master Satoshi asked.

"The Drakka attacked our city, and I went into labor," Ryoko said, her gaze distant as she recounted the terrifying moment. Kai could tell that she was reliving it all in her mind. "A dragon was struck in the sky overhead..." She paused, and Sho squeezed her hand reassuringly. "Its blood splattered all over me. We were almost to the carriage, but the pain was too much."

Ryoko's sobs echoed throughout the hall as she covered her face with her hands. Kai felt a pang in her heart as she watched her mother cry. Her own eyes welled up with tears, and one escaped, sliding down her cheek.

"The first one came easily, but something was wrong," Sho continued for her. "She was pale, and she wasn't breathing. We did everything we could, but... she was lifeless. Then Kai was born, and we had to escape. The Drakka were everywhere."

"They took her from me," Ryoko said, shuddering. "I should have fought them for her body, but I couldn't risk all of our lives for... for..."

"A corpse," Master Satoshi offered softly. "I understand."

"We left her behind," Ryoko whispered, her face haunted. "We left her behind."

Kai envisioned it all within her mind. She didn't blame her mother for leaving a child behind. As Master Satoshi said, it was a lost cause, and it would be foolish to endanger the living for the sake of the dead.

"She *is* the Blooded One," Jiro said to his brother. Kai had almost forgotten the Sworn were still present.

"There is much to consider," Master Satoshi said, ignoring Jiro's comment.

The ground trembled as a crash echoed in the courtyard. Master Satoshi exchanged glances with Liu, and the guard rushed away. He returned a moment later, his face flushed.

"The walls have been breached!"

"Impossible," Master Satoshi breathed. "Get to your dragons, now!"

The Sworn scrambled toward the courtyard, all except for Siran. She remained rooted in place. Kai looked from Master Satoshi to her parents. Her mother was still crying, but she seemed more collected now.

"Secure yourselves here in the castle," Master Satoshi told them. Turning to Kai, he stared at her in silence, his mouth twitching slightly. "You can't stay here. It's not safe without your dragon."

"I can take her to Tatenagawa," Liu said.

The shrine? Kai's brows furrowed in confusion.

"My lord!" A breathless soldier sprinted through the hall toward them. "We're surrounded! The Drakka—I've never seen so many!"

"You won't make it ten yards beyond the wall," Master Satoshi said grimly.

"Not on foot," Siran replied. "I'll take her to Tatenagawa."

"You have your orders, Siran. I will not repeat them."

"I'll take her to Tatenagawa, then go to Dangju. You can't spare anyone else, and even if you could, the others are too soft. I can take her."

"She is my charge," Liu said. "I will take her."

"You don't have a dragon," Siran countered.

"We don't have time for this," Master Satoshi snapped. "Can your dragon hold three?"

Siran's confidence wavered. "Does he have a choice?"

The sounds of battle erupted outside—the clash of metal, the roar of dragons, the screams of soldiers.

"Go," Master Satoshi conceded.

Kai embraced her mother tightly. "I will see you again," she promised.

"I'm sorry," her mother whispered.

"Don't be. It was painful for you to talk about it even now. I understand." She released her mother and turned to her father. He gave her a sad smile.

"May your blade serve you well," he said.

"You must go now," Master Satoshi urged.

Kai quickly hugged her father, then rushed toward the courtyard, following Siran. Liu was beside her, his blade drawn.

"Why are we going to Tatenagawa?" Kai asked.

"To see Kokoro," Liu replied.

"Who is that?"

"She is an elder dragon. If anyone can discern what happened here, it's her."

The three of them crossed the courtyard to where Siran's dragon waited. As they approached, the ground quaked beneath their feet as a portion of the wall collapsed. The air was thick with the acrid scent of smoke and the cries of soldiers engaged in combat.

Siran climbed onto her dragon's back, taking the frontmost position. Kai looked at Liu, who motioned for her to go next. She did so, and Liu sat behind her. Only Siran fit within the saddle, leaving Kai and Liu to sit on the rough scales of the dragon's back.

"Hold on tight," Siran said.

Kai obeyed, wrapping her arms securely around Siran's waist while Liu held onto Kai. With a powerful leap, the dragon launched into the sky, its wings beating rhythmically as it ascended higher and higher. From above, they could see the full extent of the battle unfolding below. The Drakka forces surged against the castle walls like a relentless tide.

Kai's heart raced as they soared through the air. The feeling of flight was exhilarating, but it was tainted by the events unfolding below. She worried for her parents. Ikje had never been attacked by Drakka before due to the strength of its defenses, but as she watched the dark wave of creatures overtake the walls, a chill ran down her spine.

She turned her gaze from the battle and offered a prayer to her ancestors.

CHAPTER 13

Kai focused on the landscape rushing beneath them, the fields and forests blurring together as they flew toward Tatenagawa. The wind whipped against her face, tousling her hair wildly as they cut through the air. The dragon carried them swiftly, effortlessly gliding over the terrain below.

As they approached the sacred grounds of Tatenagawa, Kai marveled at the natural beauty of the area. The lush greenery, the tranquil ponds, and the ancient trees all exuded a sense of peace and serenity. Siran's dragon descended, landing on the banks of a river where it met the ocean.

Kai dismounted after Siran, followed by Liu. The ground felt oddly solid beneath her feet after being in the air. A winding path lined with statues led to a grove of cherry blossom trees. The air was filled with the soft murmur of the river and the scent of blooming flowers. A sense of reverence washed over Kai.

"Come with me," Liu said.

"What about Siran?"

"She has her orders from Master Satoshi. She is to go to Dangju."

"If she leaves, we have no way to get back," Kai said. "What if the elder cannot help? We'll be stuck here."

"We can travel on foot if we must."

Kai looked at Siran.

"My dragon needs rest. Once he is ready, we will go. If you are not back by then, I shall see you when you return to Ikje."

Liu led Kai through the grove. Shafts of sunlight filtered through the canopy, painting patterns on the moss-covered ground. Kai noticed small shrines tucked among the trees and assumed they were offerings left by visitors. The atmosphere was tranquil, and the faint scent of incense drifted on the wind.

On the other side of the grove, a clearing opened up, revealing a grand structure. It was a temple of ancient design, its wooden beams weathered by time yet standing strong and proud. The entrance was flanked by two stone dragons that looked as if they were guarding the temple.

Liu pushed open the heavy wooden doors, and they entered a dimly lit hallway adorned with intricate murals depicting scenes of dragons soaring through the skies and warriors engaged in battle. The air was laced with the scent of sandalwood and old parchment. They walked in silence, their footsteps echoing on the polished wood floor. The hallway led them to a vast open chamber where a figure awaited them.

"Welcome," a voice greeted. The figure was cloaked in flowing robes that seemed to shift and shimmer with a life of their own. It was an elderly woman with eyes that gleamed with ancient wisdom. Her hair was silver, cascading down her back like a waterfall of moonlight. She gazed at Kai and Liu with a knowing smile, as if she had been expecting them.

"We come seeking the guidance of the elder," Liu said.

The woman's smile deepened as she studied them with a piercing gaze, her eyes seeming to see through the very core of their beings. She nodded slowly, acknowledging Liu's words.

"I had hoped this day would come before my time ended." Her voice was melodic, resonating with a power that seemed to vibrate the very air around them. "The wind whispers of you." Her eyes studied Kai. "The one who is both Chosen and not Chosen."

"As he said, we are here to see the elder," Kai said. "Will she grant us an audience?"

The woman laughed softly. "Would you rather I take my dragon form? You could not look upon me if I did. Humans are such soft creatures, even more so now than they once were."

"You are Kokoro?" Liu asked.

Kokoro nodded sagely. "I am."

"We need your help," Kai said. "Ikje is under siege by the Drakka."

"That is not why you are here. Not truly, is it? No, I think not. The wind did not lie."

Kai looked at Liu, who offered a slight nod.

"Someone stole my dragon."

"A dragon has free will," Kokoro replied. "If your dragon left, it did so of its own mind. Tell me what happened."

Kai relayed the events of the Ceremony of Oaths to her, and how her dragon said she was not his rider. She hesitated sharing her mother's revelation about birthing twins, but Liu pressed her, and she told the elder everything, including the fact her mother had been drenched in dragon's blood. Kokoro listened intently, her expression unreadable as she absorbed the tale. When Kai finished speaking, there was only silence in the chamber. Kokoro closed her eyes briefly, as if listening to some unseen force, before opening them once more.

"The threads of the world are tangled, and the path ahead is shrouded in darkness," Kokoro replied cryptically. "The balance that has long existed is unraveling. What do you know of the Accord?"

Kai shook her head. "I've never heard of it."

"And you?" Kokoro asked Liu.

"It is not familiar to me."

"That doesn't surprise me. Mankind's memory is short. Do you know how the bond came to be, or where the Drakka came from?"

Kai and Liu exchanged looks of confusion. They shook their heads in unison, prompting Kokoro to let out a soft sigh.

"The Accord is an ancient pact forged between dragons and humans centuries ago. It bound our fates together, ensuring balance and harmony in the world."

"What do you mean?" Kai asked. "Have we not always been bound to each other?"

"Before the Accord, our races were enemies. I am old enough to remember those days." Kokoro frowned. "That was a dark time. Humans are a weak species, but they outnumbered us. We called for a truce and invited the emperor to speak with us."

Kai found it hard to imagine being enemies with a dragon. They were the epitome of strength and power. The notion of dragons and humans standing on opposite sides of a battlefield seemed more akin to a fanciful tale than a history lesson.

"The emperor at the time was a wise man," Kokoro continued, her voice filled with something Kai couldn't quite place. "He saw the value in forging an alliance rather than waging war, but the price of his demand was steep. He felt dragons were too powerful, and we were forced to shed a great portion of our strength. As a result, dragons became smaller and less formidable."

Kai listened intently, her mind trying to grasp the implications of what Kokoro was revealing. The very fabric of their history was shifting, revealing secrets long buried in the sands of time.

"I cannot imagine dragons being larger than they are now," she said.

"I could show you, but I fear my transformation would burn the eyes from your skull."

"What of the Drakka? Did dragons and humans not fight them as well?"

"The Drakka did not exist," Kokoro replied. "The Accord changed the world, binding us to you in ways that are deeper than you can fathom. Some of my brethren dissented, rejecting the idea of being diminished, of bowing to human will." The elder's eyes glinted with sorrow.

"The Drakka are the remnants of my brethren who refused to abide by the terms of the Accord. With our power diminished, it had to go somewhere. It filled them until they were corrupted, becoming something entirely different. There must always be balance in the world, and the Drakka are the result of the balance correcting itself."

Kai could hardly believe what she was hearing. "The Drakka are dragons? They don't look like dragons at all."

"They once were, but as I said, they were corrupted. Now they are creatures bent on devastation. But this knowledge leads us back to you."

"Me?"

"Do you know what is written in the ancient scrolls?"

Kai shook her head. "I am not the one they speak of. I have never touched the blood of a dragon."

"Perhaps not, but it has touched you. Your mother confirmed it to you."

Kai opened her mouth to argue but as the realization settled over her, the words died in her throat. The weight of Kokoro's words bore down on Kai like a crushing wave, causing her chest to tighten. The revelation that she was somehow entwined in ancient pacts and prophecies left her reeling. She glanced at Liu, searching for a steadying presence in the swirling chaos of her thoughts. His expression mirrored her own; shock, fear, and emotions she couldn't put words to.

Kokoro's gaze lingered on Kai, the silver in her hair catching the light of the chamber like strands of moonlight woven into her being.

"Never has a dragon bonded with more than one human at once, yet the one who chose you and your sister has somehow done so. It seems your twin's connection is stronger to him than your own, but you are still Chosen. The prophecy has long been a contention among the humans. Some see it as a portent of doom, while others see it as their salvation."

"Which is it?" Kai asked, afraid to know.

"It is both."

"I don't understand. How can something be both evil and good?"

"You and your twin are two sides of the same coin. One embraces the darkness while the other shines in the light. The prophecy is not one side or the other, it is both combined."

Kai considered the elder's words. Something her mother said came back to her. "Why would the Drakka take my sister?" The words felt odd coming out of her mouth. She'd been led to believe she was an only child her entire life. "My parents thought she was dead. Why would the Drakka take a corpse?"

"The Drakka know the prophecy," Kokoro replied. "Deep down, they are dragons, and it was a dragon who penned the words. When they saw your mother covered in dragon's blood, they knew the ancient words had come to pass."

"But the Drakka are mindless creatures," Kai protested. "They couldn't know that."

Kokoro laughed. "Is that what humans tell themselves these days? The Drakka are disorganized, I will grant you. Discord is their very nature, which means they do not work together, but if someone were to unite them..."

"My sister," Kai whispered.

"Yes. The Drakka must have raised her as their own, and now she leads them. That is the only explanation for what you say is happening at Ikje. She is the dark side of the coin."

"And I am expected to be the light side?"

"I do not expect you to be anything," Kokoro said. "But you will have to make a choice. The balance that has long existed is unraveling, and it will correct itself one way or another."

"How can I do anything when I don't control the bond? The dragon said himself that Akuhara was his rider. And since I am also bound to the dragon, she can probably hear my thoughts even now."

"Perhaps, though I do not suspect the bond works that way. It is impossible to know since this has never happened before, but it does not matter."

"Why not?"

"Because you can sever your connection with him and forge a new bond."

CHAPTER 14

Kai stared at Kokoro, her brows furrowed. "I thought once a bond was formed, it only ended upon death?"

"That is usually how a bond ends, but as part of the Accord, a human reserves the right to sever it."

"What happens when the bond is severed?"

"The bond would break, and both you and the dragon would feel pain. Since you are not as connected to him as your twin, I think the pain would be lessened. You would then be free to bond with a new dragon."

"How would I bond with a new dragon? The Binding happens when we are both unborn."

"The dragon you would bond with is... unique. She is unhatched, but she has long been ready to enter the world."

The choice before her weighed heavily on her shoulders. The revelation that she could sever her bond and forge a new one with an unhatched dragon left her feeling both hopeful and terrified.

"What would I need to do to sever the bond?"

"It is not an easy task," Kokoro replied. "To sever a bond with a dragon requires great sacrifice. You must be willing to give up a part of yourself, to let go of something precious to you."

Kai's mind raced as she tried to think of what she could possibly offer. What was so important to her that ridding herself of it would be a sacrifice? Even as she considered that question, deep down she knew. She looked at Liu, who stood there silently. She wanted to ask him for guidance, but he could never understand what her choice entailed. The image of her parents came to mind, and she knew that even if her decision only saved them, it would be worth the cost.

"I will do it," she said, her voice steady despite the roiling emotions within her.

"You have a brave heart, Kai. You must go to the sacred grounds where the Accord was made. There, you will find the egg and undergo the Ritual of Severance."

"Where can I find this place?"

"It is not far from here," Kokoro answered. "I will take you there."

"I will come with you," Liu said. "Until she is Sworn, she is under my protection."

"Very well."

"We should let Siran know in case she's waiting." Kai glanced at Liu, expecting him to be annoyed that the woman was not following her orders.

"She is gone," Kokoro said.

"How do you know?"

"I felt her dragon's presence leave the area."

"Oh." Kai was disappointed, but she didn't know why. Siran had her own path to follow. Perhaps it was because she was the closest thing to a friend Kai had ever had.

"Before we go, we will eat. The journey isn't long, but it is arduous and you will need your strength for the ritual."

Kokoro treated them to a delicious meal of roasted rabbit, sweet potatoes, and an herbal tea that was both soothing and invigorating. As they ate, Kokoro talked about the Accord. The more Kai learned, the more she realized there was much she didn't know. It also made her question why no one taught them about the Accord or the history of it. Kai considered

Kokoro's words about the shortness of human memories, but she couldn't help feeling there was more to it than that.

Once they had all finished their meal, Kokoro led them out of the temple and through the grove, heading southeast to where the mountains loomed. As she had warned, the landscape was difficult to traverse. The path was rocky and uneven, and the dense forest surrounding them seemed to press in on them from all sides. The air was thick with the scent of damp leaves and earth, and the occasional rustle of small animals scurrying away revealed their presence.

Kai found herself focusing on each step, her mind racing with thoughts of the ritual ahead. They walked for several hours until, finally, they reached a clearing at the base of the mountains surrounded by ancient, towering trees that seemed to stretch towards the sky, their branches woven together like a natural cathedral. The dark entrance of a cave stood ominously before them.

"This is it," Kokoro said quietly, as if her voice could disturb the sanctity of the place.

Kai swallowed hard, feeling a strange mix of dread and anticipation.

"Are you sure about this?" Liu asked, the concern evident in his voice.

Was she? No, not really, but that didn't matter. They'd come this far, and it wouldn't be right to turn away now. She nodded.

"Come," Kokoro beckoned.

As they entered the cave, the air grew cooler. The darkness swallowed them briefly before Kokoro spoke a word Kai didn't know and torches on the walls flared to life. She led them deeper into the cave, passing strange symbols carved upon the walls. The ceiling gradually grew lower, forcing them to stoop as they walked, and the ground was covered in a thick layer of leaves.

"Time has changed this tunnel," Kokoro said. "It used to be more accommodating."

Despite the light of the torches, the darkness seemed to pull at Kai, and she gripped the hilt of her sword for comfort, her heart racing. The cave curved inward, twisting and turning like a maze. Kokoro led them deeper still until the tunnel opened up into a vast chamber, hollowed out of the mountain's heart.

In the center sat a massive egg, its surface a deep shade of gold with iridescent markings that sparkled like stars against the blackness of the chamber. Kai's breath caught in her throat. It was the most beautiful thing she had ever seen. She couldn't tear her eyes away from it, and she could sense the dormant life pulsating from the egg. As they drew closer, Kai realized the egg towered over all of them. It seemed too large to belong to a dragon. She glanced at Liu, but his focus was captured by the golden egg.

"It's so big," Kai whispered.

"As I said, this dragon is unique. Now, to sever your bond, you will place your hands upon the egg and envision your *ki*. Find the connection that flows outward from it toward your dragon and cut it using your sacrifice as the blade."

Kai nodded and quietly approached the egg. The energy coming from the egg stirred, and she could feel something brush against her mind. Was this what her mother had experienced during the Binding? She pushed the thought away and laid her hands on the egg. The surface was smooth and radiated warmth.

Closing her eyes, she focused on her *ki*. In her mind's eye, she found the bond and pictured it as a glowing thread linking her to the gray dragon. With a deep breath, she summoned her courage. She had never wanted to be Chosen. Instead, she had wanted an easy life, one filled with children of her own. Tears stung her eyes as she imagined her motherhood as a blade and placed it against the thread. Steeling herself, she cut the bond.

A searing pain shot through her, causing her to gasp and lose her balance. Liu moved swiftly to support her, but Kokoro gestured for him to stay back.

"She must endure this on her own," she said.

Gritting her teeth, Kai pushed through the pain, focusing on cutting the bond cleanly and completely. The golden egg beneath her hands began to resonate with her efforts, its surface pulsating with a soft light. With one final surge of willpower, Kai felt the connection snap, causing a wave of agony to ripple through her entire being.

Her legs threatened to give out, but she clung stubbornly to her resolve, the darkness at the edge of her vision almost within reach. Through the storm of pain, she felt the egg begin to quiver. As the pain subsided, Kai started to breathe again, her hands trembling against the egg. She had done it. The bond was severed.

"Now forge the new bond," Kokoro urged.

Kai took a deep breath, her heart pounding in her chest. She knew what she had to do, but she couldn't shake the feeling of loss.

"How do I...?" she began, but Kokoro interrupted her.

"Feel the connection that pulses between you and the egg. Envision it as a stream of living energy, flowing from you to the egg and back again. Your *ki* is essential to forging the bond."

Kai felt the energy Kokoro spoke of. She closed her eyes and concentrated, visualizing her *ki*. She reached out with it, feeling it flow towards the egg. The connection took shape, a golden thread linking the two of them together.

The egg responded to her efforts, emitting a soft hum that seemed to resonate with the very depths of her soul. Kai could sense a presence awakening within the golden shell, a consciousness stirring to life. It was unlike anything she had ever experienced, a merging of minds that transcended words or thoughts.

In that moment of unity, Kai felt a surge of emotions wash over her—joy, acceptance, and a profound sense of belonging. The golden thread shimmered and brightened, signifying the strength of their connection. A wave of dizziness washed over her, and as her vision darkened, she could hear Liu's voice, distant and echoing.

CHAPTER 15

As Kai's eyelids fluttered open, she found herself sprawled on the ground in front of the egg. She sat up and noticed Liu and Kokoro gazing down at her. Liu's face was creased with worry, while Kokoro's radiated a sense of pride.

"The Binding is complete," the elder said.

Kai looked at the egg. The energy pulsing from within it was no longer dormant. It was active, and she could feel a presence within her mind, almost like her conscience, yet it was separate from her.

"When will it hatch?" Kai asked.

As if in answer to her question, a soft rumble resonated from the egg. It grew in intensity until cracks spiderwebbed across the egg's surface, emitting a soft golden light that illuminated the chamber in a dazzling display. Kai watched in awe as the dragon hatchling emerged from the egg, its scales gleaming like molten gold. It was just as large as the ones from the ceremony.

The dragon blinked its large, brilliant blue eyes and fixed them on Kai with an expression that seemed to convey wisdom beyond its years. It extended its snout towards her, nuzzling her hand in a gesture of trust and companionship. Tears welled up in Kai's eyes as she realized the depth of the connection she now shared with this majestic creature. The dragon's presence in her mind felt both strange and comforting, like a familiar voice speaking to her from a place deep within her soul.

Kai reached out tentatively, running her hand along the dragon hatchling's scales, feeling the warmth that radiated from its body. It chirruped softly, a sound that tugged at Kai's heartstrings. She could sense the dragon's curiosity and intelligence, and a flash of images appeared within her mind, and she realized it was trying to communicate with her.

I am Kai Lin, she said, sending the words through their bond.

More images flashed through her mind's eye, but she couldn't decipher their meaning.

"She can't speak?" Kai asked, looking at Kokoro.

"Not yet. Much like a human, it takes time to grow. Your dragon will mature faster than other dragons, and through your bond, you will help her learn about our world."

"You said she was unique. What does that mean?"

Kokoro glanced at Liu, and Kai assumed she didn't want to answer in front of him. "Whatever you want to tell me you can say in front of him," Kai said. "I trust him."

"Very well. Your dragon is different because she is an elder."

"Like you?"

"Yes."

"That's forbidden," Liu said.

"I know. I was there when the Accord was written."

"Then why did you allow this?"

"There are countless reasons, but I will tell you the most important one." Kokoro's demeanor grew solemn. "I am the sole survivor of my species. Well, not anymore," she gestured towards the golden dragon. "But my days are numbered. I will dedicate the remainder of my life to training both of you. When I am gone, your dragon will be the final elder. It will be her responsibility to ensure our kind lives on."

"You used me?" Kai's face flushed with heat, both in surprise and anger. Her dragon growled, mirroring her emotions.

"No. Dragons do not employ such tactics. You and your sister are the ones written of, but the prophecy is not for humans... it is for dragons. The Accord took our power, but you will give it back to us."

Taking a deep breath to steady herself, Kai reached out and gently stroked the dragon's scales. The bond between them pulsed with newfound energy, a connection that seemed to grow stronger with each passing moment. Despite the circumstances surrounding their union, Kai had a feeling deep down that she was meant to walk this path. Whether she wanted to was another matter entirely.

Fate or destiny had called upon her, that much was clear, and she couldn't deny the sense of purpose that stirred within her. As she looked into the wise blue eyes of her dragon companion, she knew that their fates were intertwined in ways she was only beginning to understand. She straightened, determination shining in her gaze.

"I cannot guarantee I will fulfill this prophecy, if I am even truly the one it speaks if, but I will do whatever I must to protect my dragon and both of our species," Kai said. The dragon regarded her with a knowing look, as if understanding the weight of her words. Kokoro smiled, the darkness leaving her expression.

"You have the heart of a true dragon rider. Remember, the bond between you and your dragon is not just about duty. It is about trust, understanding, and love." With those words lingering in the air, Kokoro turned to Liu. "You no longer need to protect her. She is my ward now, and no harm will come to her."

"I mean no insult, but I made an oath to defend the Chosen I am assigned to until my last breath or until they are Sworn. If I do not keep my oath, my words mean nothing and I have no honor."

"Your honor is not in question," Kokoro said softly, her voice full of compassion. "But sometimes, the path we tread deviates from the one we have set for ourselves. Kai's journey is no longer yours to safeguard. She has taken the first step towards fulfilling a destiny greater than any single oath. You are welcome to stay here while she trains, but they must grow their bond in solitude, away from prying eyes."

"I understand," Liu replied. "I will not pry nor get in the way of her training."

"Thank you." Kokoro turned her attention back to Kai. "There is much for you to learn, and time is of the essence. Your dragon is an elder, and while she carries the wisdom of our ancestors within her, you must learn to communicate with her, to understand her thoughts and feelings. This will not be easy, but I will guide you through the process."

Kai nodded. She was ready for the challenges that lay ahead, ready to forge a bond unlike any the world had ever seen before. The dragon chirruped softly, nudging her hand with its snout as if agreeing with her. Kai could feel the weight of responsibility settling on her shoulders, but for the first time in her life, she no longer felt like she was facing things alone.

"First things first," Kai said. "You need a name."

TO BE CONTINUED IN...
ACOLYTE

Did you enjoy this book?

    If so, you'll probably like my others. You'll find a preview of some of my other works on the following pages.

    Thank you for reading this one, and I hope you look forward to the next one!

A Preview of Trial by Sorcery

I marveled at the vastness of the Citadel.

It was home to the Dragon Guard, the greatest warriors of the kingdom. While that was impressive alone, it was made even more amazing because it was also the home of dragons. The massive, powerful creatures were kept in the lower chamber of the castle. At least, that's what my father used to tell me.

A wall forty feet high surrounded the city of Autumnwick, as well as the stone fortress that towered behind it. This was my first time seeing the place, and it was just as large and imposing as I'd always imagined it to be. The massive gates that provided entrance through the wall were manned with guards armed to the teeth. A small line had formed at the entrance as the guards checked everyone entering.

I traveled downhill and joined the line, adjusting my sword belt. The weight of the blade continuously pulled down on my pants. It made me reconsider my decision to use a side sheath instead of one that went over the shoulder. It was too late to change my mind now. I'd spent the last of my coins to reach the Citadel, and I doubted the school would allow me to carry a blade during my training anyway.

The line shuffled forward slowly. I did my best to remain patient, but it was difficult. I was finally here! The home of the Dragon Guard! I'd dreamed of joining their ranks for as long as I could remember. My father's stories had always been filled with awe and wonder as he described his dragon and the bond they shared.

Although it was still early in the day, the sky was clear and the sun beat down mercilessly. I could feel droplets of sweat running down my back and sides. I drank the last of the water in my canteen and continued to wait. After what felt like an eternity of baking in the sun, I was next for inspection. I glanced behind me and saw the line was much longer now. There were at least a hundred people waiting to get into the city.

"Hold it there, low born," one of the guards said.

I looked ahead, thinking he was speaking to me. He wasn't. His attention was on a girl in front of me with long black hair. They'd already given her sack a thorough check, but the one talking grabbed her by the elbow and pulled her aside. I couldn't hear what he was saying to her because he'd lowered his voice, but whatever it was, the girl did not look amused.

"You, stop gawking and get over here."

The other guard was glaring at me. I hurried forward. The guard looked me up and down and frowned.

"What's your business?" he asked.

"I'm here to sign up for the school," I answered, trying to ignore the sweat sliding down my back. The other guard was still speaking with the girl, and he was being a little too touchy in my opinion.

"Another low born seeking fame and riches, huh?"

The guard was wearing a helm, but the ends of his hair sticking out from under it were blond. He was a high born, a noble. They were all the same. They thought they were better than everyone else simply because they were born with a different shade of hair color. I'd been bullied in my hometown a few times, not just for my social standing, and I knew in a city this size that it would be much worse.

The problem with this guard, however, was that he was only paying attention to my hair. He clearly didn't notice the insignia that was sewn into my upper sleeve. I didn't like to flounce it, but sometimes it was fun to bring a noble down a peg or two.

"Stop it," the girl with the other guard shouted. He'd pulled her close and was trying to kiss her. I'd seen enough. I turned my body so that the guard could see my insignia and smiled at him. His eyes widened for a brief moment, then he collected himself and waved me through.

"Apologies," he muttered.

I nodded at him, still smiling, and walked over to where the other guard was harassing the girl.

"Is there a problem, cousin?" I asked.

Both the girl and the guard looked at me. The girl was confused and the guard looked irritated.

"I figured you would have been lost in the market by now," I said to the girl. I was hoping she would catch on to what I was doing and play along. She tilted her head ever so slightly as a wordless sign of thanks and stepped back from the guard.

"I'm fine," she huffed. "This gentleman was just telling me how to get to the school."

"How kind of you, sir," I said, showing off my insignia to him as well. He looked at it, then looked me in the eyes. He hated that he couldn't stop me. I could see the seething anger in his blue eyes.

"Would you mind repeating the directions? My cousin is terrible at remembering things like that. Aren't you, cousin?"

I exchanged glances with the girl. She shrugged. "What can I say? I'm not used to doing things on my own."

The guard glowered at me. Through clenched teeth, he said, "Go straight. Through the market. When you reach the wall, turn right. The entrance is on the left."

Before I could antagonize him further, he stomped past me and returned to his post with the other guard.

"A bit of a jerk, that one," I said. The girl was already through the gate, leaving me talking to myself. I followed her and had to walk twice as fast to catch up.

"I'm Eldwin," I said.

"Go away," the girl replied.

"I'm sorry, I thought I just helped you back there."

The girl stopped and turned around, placing her hands on her hips and giving me a death stare.

"Did I ask for your help?"

"No …"

"Do I look like some sort of helpless wench that needs rescue?" she demanded.

"Uh, no …"

"That's because I'm not," she growled. "I can take care of myself."

"Sorry," I said lamely, putting my hands up. Her eyes widened slightly at the sight of my right hand. "I didn't mean to upset you. I just thought … never mind. Forget that I said or did anything."

I walked past her and continued following the road. The girl's response to seeing my mangled hand was the same as everyone else who saw it. Horror, disgust, you name it. It came as no surprise to me anymore.

The buildings on either side were short and squat, all of them built with a dull gray stone. The buildings on the right ended after several feet and opened into a large space filled with vendors. Multicolored tents were arranged in orderly rows and delicious scents filled the air, making my mouth water. My stomach growled and I absently patted it.

My breakfast had been filling, but I'd walked the last few miles to Autumnwick and now I was hungry. Considering I didn't have any money for food, I was hoping the school would provide meals. My father had never told me about his training days, so I wasn't sure what awaited me.

All the sights and smells temporarily distracted my mind from the girl, who I found to be quite pretty. Her attitude, on the other hand, made me question my judgment. I watched the various vendors as they stood under their tents, hawking their wares and trying to negotiate prices with potential customers. The sun seemed to grow hotter by the second as I stood there. I wiped the back of my hand across my forehead and was about to continue to the school when the girl walked up to me.

"I'm sorry," she huffed.

"Don't worry about it," I said.

"No, really. I didn't mean to be rude. It's just …" she trailed off and looked down. "My whole life, people have tried to help me for their own gain. I've made it a point in my life to never need help from anyone."

What she said didn't make any sense. She was a low born like me, so what would anyone have to gain by helping her? I pushed the thought away.

"Apology accepted," I said. "I didn't mean to offend you or anything. I thought that guard was being a little forceful for his own good and thought I could help diffuse the situation."

"Thank you," she said. She paused a moment, then said, "I'm Maren."

Maren. That was different ... but beautiful.

"Nice to meet you, Maren," I said. "Are you really going to the school?"

"I am," Maren confirmed. "I want to be a Dragon Guard."

"So do I," I said. "My father was one."

"Was?"

"He died," I answered. "In a big battle ten years ago."

Maren's eyed widened. "Wait. Your father was Matthias Baines?"

I nodded. "That's how I got this," I pointed to the insignia on my sleeve. "Noble by Deed."

She stared at the patch intently for a moment, then turned toward the market. "Something smells good," she said. "Want to help me find what it is?"

I wanted to say yes, but because I didn't have any money, I was forced to decline. Thankfully, she didn't ask for a reason. I wouldn't have lied to her if she had, but I would have been embarrassed. My father's heroics may have earned my family a noble title, but that title didn't come with riches.

"I'll see you at the school," I said.

Maren shrugged and disappeared into the crowded marketplace. A droplet of sweat

threatened to drip into my eye and I wiped it
away, then continued toward the Citadel.

Girls were odd creatures.

A Preview of Scale of the Dragon

The sun glared overhead, reminding Mina why she dreaded Lord Klodian's summer hunting trips. He was almost obsessive in his desire to hunt dragons for sport, and he used Mina like a hound to sniff them out.

Her life hadn't always been so exciting. Once, she'd been a normal girl that worked the farm with her family ... until they sold her to Lord Klodian. Those days seemed so long ago now. At least the memories no longer brought her to tears. She'd cried enough to last her the rest of her life, as far as she was concerned.

"Which way, girl?"

Mina's pace had slowed, prompting Lord Klodian's demand. She looked over her shoulder at him. He sat astride his black warhorse, his polished plate armor glinting in the sunlight. The visor of his helm was up, and he glared at her impatiently.

To his right rode a group of his retainers, and on his left was Vhan, Klodian's squire. The retainers stared at her with a bored expression plastered on their faces, but Vhan looked excited. The squire was always thrilled when it came to dragon hunts.

"This way," Mina replied.

She continued trudging along the dunes, following the subtle pull she felt from the scale embedded in her leg. It infuriated her that Klodian forced her to walk while he and his entourage got to ride horses. Certainly, he knew it would be quicker if she were mounted, but then again, he probably did it just to spite her.

Mina was Klodian's slave, and she knew it. Whether or not it was legal was another issue, but from what Mina had gathered so far in her young life, Dominion Lords did whatever pleased them so long as it didn't get them into trouble with the High Prince.

She supposed it was a small blessing to belong to Klodian. There were rumors that other Dominion Lords could be very abusive, violent even. While Klodian had never raised a hand toward her, he was manipulative and impetuous. Growing up amidst the wealthy and elite seemed to breed those qualities into people, though.

Ahead, Mina spotted a tall mesa that rose several hundred feet above the surrounding landscape. The top was flat, and the sides were steep and straight as if some underground creature had pushed it directly up out of the ground. The rock formation was various shades of red all intermingled, but that wasn't what caught Mina's attention.

It was the shadowed cave entrance.

She angled her steps toward the mountain and the scale in her leg began to burn. It was only slightly uncomfortable, but once they got within a few hundred feet of the dragon, the pain would be excruciating. It happened every time, but that never stopped her. It wasn't the fear that Klodian would punish her that kept her from turning away. It was her hatred for dragons.

They were the source of her misery. Or rather, one of them was. That didn't matter to Mina. The only good dragon was a dead one, and so she would continue to lead Lord Klodian on his hunts with the hope that—one day—he would kill the beast whose scale made her life a nightmare.

"It's there," Mina said. "Inside the cave."

"You're certain?" Klodian asked. "It's not on top, preparing to swoop down on us?"

She turned to regard him. Klodian hadn't kept his title as Dominion Lord for no reason. He'd been born to the position, certainly, but that didn't guarantee someone the title for life. There was always some young upstart who wanted the power and fame for themselves, and Klodian's quick wits and suspicion had saved him from many assassination attempts.

"I'm certain, my Lord. The scale may be a curse, but it never lies."

"One man's curse is another man's godsend. You may not like your ability, girl, but your gift has increased my wealth fourfold."

That was another thing that bothered Mina. Lord Klodian always referred to her as 'girl' and never by her actual name. She supposed he did that out of spite, as well.

"You are entitled to your opinion, as am I. And I say it is a curse."

Klodian laughed and slid off his mount, landing with a clatter as his plate mail jounced about. He unsheathed his sword from his waistbelt and quickly looked it over, then returned it. He motioned to Vhan, and the squire also dismounted. Vhan carried a spear, but the weapon wasn't his. He hadn't earned the privilege of learning to fight yet.

"Wait for me out here," Klodian ordered, taking the spear from Vhan. "I'll be back shortly."

Mina watched him disappear inside the cave. The retainers began talking amongst themselves, sharing gossip and discussing things that made Mina wish a dragon would swoop down on them. Whether it ate them or her didn't matter, so long as it put her out of her misery.

Vhan slowly sidled around to where Mina stood, a grin on his face.

"Don't even ask," Mina said.

"I've never seen it," Vhan replied. "And I *really* want to see it."

"Why? So you can make fun of me, too? No, thank you."

"I wouldn't make fun of you. I think having a dragon scale in your leg is neat. I'd have one if I could. How did you get that, anyway?"

"I'm sure you've heard the stories," Mina said.

"I've heard rumors, which is usually far from the truth. And I've never heard the story from you, so …"

Vhan stared at her expectantly.

"I fell on it."

"Care to elaborate?"

Mina heaved a sigh, knowing Vhan would irritate her until she gave in.

"I was playing in the hills when I was young, and a hole opened up beneath me. I fell into a dragon's nest and landed on a pile of scales. This one," Mina slapped her thigh, "happened to penetrate my skin."

Vhan's eyes were wide. "Seriously? That must have been amazing. Being in a dragon's nest, I mean."

"The nest was abandoned. And it wasn't amazing at all. It ruined my life."

"You're alive, aren't you?" Vhan asked.

"I exist, but I wouldn't exactly call being a slave to Klodian living."

"Some people don't like him, but I do. He's always nice to me. I have a warm bed and food to eat, so I can't complain. There wasn't much to go around at my home, so being the squire to Lord Klodian has been the best thing that's happened to me."

Mina offered him a fake smile in the hopes that he'd get the hint and stop talking, but he kept yammering on about how great it was to be part of Klodian's Dominion. Mina tuned his voice out and watched the cave entrance, wondering how long it would take Klodian to kill the dragon. Her leg was still burning, which meant it wasn't dead yet. At least he hadn't forced them to go into the cave with him.

After a while, Vhan left her alone and wandered over to listen to the retainers. Mina rubbed her leg, massaging the skin around the edges of the scale. She didn't fear for Klodian's safety. If he died, then she'd have an opportunity to escape. It wasn't likely he'd be killed, though. Not when he had the power of his runes. That was another perk the wealthy nobles enjoyed: magic.

Rune magic was sanctioned by the High Prince, and it was only lawful for nobles to employ it. Everything else was outlawed, but that didn't stop people from practicing it in secret. Although Mina had never met any illegal sorcerers, she knew they were out there. It was whispered that on the fringes of the Dominions, there were people who openly sold their services to others.

The burning in Mina's leg ceased abruptly, and she smiled. Another dragon was dead. *Good riddance,* she thought. A moment later, Lord Klodian stepped out from the cave. He was covered in dust and blood, and he carried a severed horn in one hand. Vhan rushed over and fawned over him, ever the loyal squire. Mina found the display annoying and turned her gaze away, looking up at the mesa's jagged walls.

"That's the first dragon of the season," Vhan said.

"The first of many," Klodian replied. "Girl."

Mina looked at him, and he tossed the horn to her. She caught it and turned it over, examining it. It was small, and she guessed the dragon must have been an adolescent.

"For your collection," Klodian said.

"Thank you, my Lord."

"Ride back to the castle and summon the workers," Klodian instructed Vhan. "Tell them to bring plenty of wagons. The beast was hoarding enough trinkets to fund an army."

"Right away, sir."

Vhan got on his horse and rode off. The retainers gathered around Klodian and listened to him relay how he killed the dragon. Mina ran her fingers along the horn, feeling the coarse lines that grooved its surface. Every horn was different, but they all had similarities. She glanced at the cave and thought she saw glowing eyes staring back at her from the shadows. She blinked a few times and squinted, but there was nothing there.

It was probably her imagination. She waited for Klodian to finish bragging about his kill, and then they began the trek back to the castle. Mina clutched the horn in her hands, hoping that the next dragon to be killed would be the one to set her free.

How she hated dragons.

When rumors of a dragon attack reached Demetrius, he dismissed them almost immediately. Having lived in the port city of Radda his entire life, he had heard many wild stories from countless travelers. Everything ranging from giant squids in the open seas to horses with wings. Admittedly this *was* the first time he heard mention of a dragon, supposed giant mythical creatures that fed on the fear of people and could lay waste to entire cities.

"Rubbish," he said. "Children's tales told by parents to scare little ones into obedience."

"I believe it," the old sailor remarked enthusiastically. "Captain heard it 'imself. Says the whole city was burned to the ground and everyone killed."

"Then how did your captain hear of it?" Demetrius eyed his friend sternly. The man's face was covered in wrinkles and his hair bleached from constant sun. The man had been a sailor since he was not more than a boy and was prone to believe almost anything.

"What d'ya mean?" the sailor, Bannigan, asked.

"If everyone was killed, how did your captain hear this story? Who would have repeated it to him?"

The old man remained silent for a moment and scratched his prickly-haired chin. "It not be my place to question the Captain, silversmith."

Demetrius laughed heartily. "Nice cover up."

The sailor stomped his foot indignantly. "It ain't no cover up. I trust the Captain's word. How's business?" Bannigan changed the subject.

"Profitable, as always. The war with Oakvalor hasn't put a pinch in anyone's pockets yet. I hear some of my fellow smiths have been requested to appear before the king, as to why is anyone's guess."

"Maybe the king needs more weapons."

Demetrius shrugged his large shoulders. He wasn't in the business of making weapons, so it mattered little to him. His craft was typically sought after by the well-to-do, custom pieces that didn't come cheap. Some people had so much money they apparently didn't know what to do with it. He could work with any metal he put his hands on, but he preferred silver. It was very easy to bend and could be cast or hammered which allowed him to form almost anything with it; from teapots to statues.

The clanging of the bell tower echoed loudly across the city, signaling noon. The bell tower was originally built to alert the populace of emergencies. Its main use now was to indicate the time. Bannigan clapped Demetrius on the shoulder and bid him farewell. "That's my call," he said, trying to be heard over the noise. Demetrius' shop was situated near the docks for convenience and the daily clanging of the bell had eventually become a normal sound to him.

"Be safe," he called out as the old man left. Bannigan waved to acknowledge he heard him. Not that anyone couldn't.

Demetrius was a large man with a thunderous voice. At six and a half feet tall, he was a beast of a man, with muscles so large that he had to be custom fitted for his clothing. His hair was light brown and cut short to keep it out of his eyes, and to keep it from being singed. His skin was a deep bronze color as he preferred to be in the sun most of his time.

He watched his friend until he could no longer see him among the crowd. He heard his name a few stalls down and glanced to see who said it. He could see a member of the king's guard talking to one of the vendors. The vendor pointed towards where he was standing. What in the Divines would a soldier of the crown want with him? He watched the soldier approach.

"Demetrius?"

The big man eyed the soldier warily. "Yes?"

"The silversmith?" he asked with an air of impatience.

"Yes."

The soldier withdrew a scroll from his belt and handed it to Demetrius. "What's this?" he questioned. The soldier shook his head. "Not my business, sir. I am just the messenger. I believe His Highness requests your presence at the palace."

"What for?" Demetrius probed.

"Not my business." The soldier's impatience was evident by his short, almost rude, answers. "I must be on my way, sir." The soldier turned and headed back from the way he came. Demetrius stared at the scroll, unsure if he even wanted to open it. Everyone knew he didn't make weapons. Why would the king summon him if he was seeking smiths to make his armies more weapons?

He snapped the seal in half and opened the scroll. It read:

To Demetrius the silversmith,

There was a fancy signature and the crest of the king, a phoenix bursting forth from a pile of ashes, at the bottom of the parchment. Demetrius sighed. He hated politics.

Dusk found him standing near the road at the outskirts of his hometown. He had closed up his shop early much to his disappointment. There was a certain beautiful woman who walked by his stall everyday around the same time, usually carrying fresh bread. He had only noticed her because he caught her staring at him as she passed by one day.

Her look was one of admiration. At least, that's how he took it. She had smiled embarrassedly and blushed. And so Demetrius made it a point in his day to watch her as she walked by and smile at her.

Closing early meant that he missed her.

He was more than slightly frustrated by that, as he had finally worked up his nerve to actually speak to her. His hope was that she would let him get to know her and perhaps they would see where things went from there.

The carriage pulled up suddenly and Demetrius noticed that the sun was just sliding behind the mountains. "Well at least the king is punctual," he muttered beneath his breath. The door to the carriage swung open and a man dressed in plain clothes, probably a servant, stepped out. He motioned to the carriage and bowed low. "If you would, sir."

Demetrius dipped his head in thanks and climbed inside. A quiet whistle escaped his lips. The inside was adorned with all sorts of glittering shapes. He looked closely and recognized most of the precious stones. Diamonds and rubies comprised most of the decorations, but there were also a few sapphires and a couple stones he did not recognize. The fabric that made up the seats was comfortable and smooth to the touch. It was hard to tell whether the material was dark red or brown in the fading light.

Demetrius was impressed. He didn't expect to be brought to the palace in luxury. Granted he was known among the higher ups for his skills in crafting, but he was not of noble birth. And most, if not all of them, seemed to ignore the fact that he was much wealthier than most of them, anyway. The servant did not get back into the carriage, but instead shut the door and climbed into the seat with the driver.

He had a decent amount of time to think as the buggy headed toward Tarvaarin, the city built around the palace. It was a thirty-minute trip to the palace by horse. After what seemed like hours to him, he felt a difference in the road. Instead of bouncing about on the dirt path, the ride smoothed out and he could tell they were now on the stone paved roads of the city.

The carriage came to an abrupt stop and the door swung open. The servant stood there and motioned for Demetrius to come out. He had gotten comfortable and it took him a minute to move. Why did the king want him to come so late in the evening hours, he wondered.

The servant led him through enormously tall double doors and into a massive circular room that was normally filled with nobles and commoners alike, usually bringing petitions and requests to the king or his advisors. The room was empty and their footsteps reverberated off the walls.

Demetrius looked admiringly up at the vaulted ceiling, rising sixty feet above him. Support pillars were spaced every ten feet, outlining the main walkway through the antechamber. "This is huge," he remarked to himself.

"Sir?" the servant looked back at him. Demetrius shook his head and the servant continued his hurried pace. A door in the middle of the far wall was flanked on either side by two giant alabaster statues of winged men standing at attention, their swords drawn and held up before them. Demetrius thought them an odd addition to the room. The walls were covered with portraits of regal looking men, whom he assumed were previous kings, and large brightly colored tapestries depicting scenes of long ago battles.

He began to wonder why he had never made a trip to the palace, if for no other reason than to say he had been there. The servant stopped before the door. "Wait here, sir," he said breathlessly before disappearing through the door. Demetrius looked down at the floor. Stone tiles, painted orange and yellow, ran the length of the entire room, forming a triangular pattern. The tiles outside the three-sided shape were bright red.

He assumed there was some sort of significance to the design, but it was lost on him. Demetrius looked back up and noticed the servant was staring at him. "His Highness will see you now." He held the door open and pointed down a long hallway. "It's the last door on the left at the end of the hall."

The big man nodded his head in thanks and walked to where he was directed. The hallway, large enough to comfortably hold two carriages side by side, was barely adorned at all. A guard stepped out from the shadows and startled him. "I didn't see you," he laughed nervously.

"That would be the point," the guard answered, his face hidden by the hood over his head. He patted Demetrius down for weapons and finding none, opened the door for him to enter. "Go to the center of the room and do not leave the circle."

"Circle? Why not?"

"Just don't."

Demetrius was starting to regret having made the trip. Then again, seeing how guarded the king was, he doubted he would have lived long had he refused to come. He walked to the middle of the room and noticed the circle design in the floor. He assumed that's where he was supposed to stand.

The guard shut the door and Demetrius was enveloped in darkness. He cleared his throat and the sound echoed eerily. Torches flared to life and revealed a large wooden chair with a man seated on it.

"Demetrius," the unknown man greeted. "I don't think we've had the pleasure of meeting before."

Demetrius wasn't sure if it was the king or not. And if it was, should he bow? He didn't answer. The man must have took his lack of response as hesitance. "You can speak freely."

Demetrius felt a little better that he could speak his mind. He wasn't one to bite his tongue. "What is this about? Why am I here? I am a very busy man, and I have lost half a day's time—"

The man in the chair stood up swiftly and Demetrius fell silent. "I can assure you, master smith, that we are all busy. Some busy with tasks more important than others." The man tossed a leather pouch onto the floor in front of him. "Consider this payment for your time."

Demetrius didn't dare move from the circle to see what was inside, heeding the warning the guard had given him.

"Talvaard has a shadow cast over it, master smith. A shadow that threatens to consume us all."

Demetrius assumed the shadow was Oakvalor, the enemy kingdom that Talvaard had been at war with for as long as anyone could remember. "Then I must inform you, sir, that I am not a weapon smith. I make trinkets and items ordered for noble houses. I think you have erred in your selection of men to build your weapons of war."

"Do you think that I am ignorant of those in my kingdom?" the man asked, revealing that he was indeed the king. "I know what you are capable of, Demetrius, and I have not summoned you here to build weapons. At least, not in the sense that you are thinking."

"What do you mean?"

Several other torches lit up, as though by magic, and exposed King Garun in all his splendor. He was shorter than Demetrius by at least a foot. His hair was long and black, pulled back tight into a ponytail. His nose slanted down his face, reminding Demetrius of a bird's beak. His eyes were hazel and set deep in his head. The king was nothing special in terms of attractiveness. What he lacked in looks, however, was made up for in bearing.

His posture and demeanor exhibited a great deal of confidence and his general appearance was enhanced by his garments. His crown gleamed in the torchlight and gave the impression that it was made of silver. Demetrius knew it wasn't crafted of his favorite metal, but was instead made of something much more valuable: white gold.

It had three gems set in the front. A rare black diamond, twenty karats by Demetrius' estimate, in the middle, surrounded on either side by two green serendibite stones. It was a marvelous treasure. The king's shirt was turquoise and had a lustrous, dazzling sheen that only silk could give. His linen pants were a brilliant green color tucked into black leather boots. During the daylight hours, when dealing with matters of state, he would also wear a mantle that extended to the floor, joined at the neck and open down the front, that was emblazoned with the large phoenix crest on the back.

"I'm sure you have heard the rumors?"

"Of dragons, Your Highness?"

"Indeed. I can read the disbelief in your face. I know how you feel, as I too was of the same mind when word first reached me. I can assure you," the king's tone grew somber, "there is no myth to these tales."

Demetrius was dubious. "What in the name of the Divines are you talking about?

Dragons? Winged creatures that fly and breath fire? You can't be serious, Your Highness."

The king's face remained solemn. "Had I not seen the creature for myself, I would be as doubtful as you, Demetrius. Unfortunately," he paused, gave a great sigh, and continued, "it is very real."

Demetrius was still in doubt, but he didn't further voice his suspicion. "What does all this have to do with me?"

"It is said that no one in Talvaard can work silver like you."

Demetrius had certainly earned a strong reputation for himself, but he was down to earth and didn't like to boast. "So I have heard," he replied, shrugging his large shoulders. "You still haven't answered the question."

The king closed the distance between him and Demetrius with a few quick steps. "I cannot reveal the details just yet, as I myself do not have them. All I know is that the skills of a silversmith are required, along with a few other details. Our ally," he used the word frostily, "does not have the privilege of metal smiths. And we lack what they have. So you see, master smith, you would be doing Talvaard a great duty."

"And if I refuse?" Demetrius asked, more out of curiosity than rebelliousness. A job for the king could prove to be very profitable.

Garun eyed him dangerously. "It would not be in your best interest ... but you have a week to consider it."

Demetrius felt goose bumps run up his back under the king's baleful look. "I am loyal to my country, Your Highness. I would never refuse an opportunity to serve the crown."

Garun smiled, the first Demetrius had seen on his face, apparently pleased with the answer. "My servant will escort you out and deliver you back to your home."

"When will you require my services?"

"You will know," the king answered.

A Preview of Throne of Deceit

The Seven Stars inn was busier than normal.

That was good for business, but it also meant that Gwen had been rushing around most of the evening, filling tankards and delivering steaming food. It was warm, uncomfortably so, and Gwen was glad the night was almost over. The air was thick with pipe smoke and boisterous laughter, a rarity these days.

Gwen spotted a man waving his arm, tankard upside down on the table. She heaved a weary sigh and hurried to the table, forcing a smile.

"More ale?" she asked.

"Yes, and keep it flowing," the man replied.

Gwen could tell by the way he slurred his words that he'd probably already had too much, but she nodded and refilled his tankard. The inn would be closing soon, so not much more ale would be "flowing" anyway. Gwen's father had been in the kitchen since opening, fulfilling the endless stream of orders and cursing when he burned himself, which was quite often.

A bard began playing a cheerful song, his fingers flying over the strings of his lute with a practiced ease. Gwen liked the melodies he played, but he was passing through and tonight would be his last performance at the inn. She did another loop of the tables, making sure the patrons were taken care of, then sat behind the bar and listened to the music.

Gwen found the bard handsome. He was young and energetic, his face clean shaven, and his brown hair trimmed short and neat. Her father would never allow her to marry someone with a profession that required constant travel, but she didn't see any problem with admiring the man's attractiveness. Besides that, it was common knowledge that Gwen would take over the Seven Stars once her father retired.

As the bard finished his song, a commotion outside the inn caught Gwen's attention. She looked to the windows, but it was too dark to see anything other than vague shadows. The noise drew the attention of the inn's customers as well, and the people quickly congregated in front of the windows. Those who couldn't squeeze in among the others exited the doors to see things up close.

Gwen heard angry shouting and groaned. Drunken men fist fighting one another wasn't uncommon, especially when the place was busy. She removed her apron and hung it on one of the hooks on the wall, then walked to the door and cracked it open, peering out into the night.

A single man was surrounded by a group of the king's soldiers. Their black leather armor made them blend in with the darkness, but Gwen knew the attire. The soldiers had become a common sight around the inn, and around Dawsbury in general. Rumors of war had been circulating for years, but now there were signs of it. Aside from the presence of the king's men, there were also whispers of dark magic and sightings of dragons.

Gwen didn't know what to think about any of it. She lived a simple life working at the inn, and she wanted it to stay that way. The king could make war on the surrounding kingdoms if he wanted to, so long as Gwen's way of life wasn't impacted. Her attention was jerked back to the present when one of the soldiers kicked the back of the man's legs, knocking him to the ground. The man being harassed scowled and tried to get back up.

"Stay down, dog," one of the soldiers said.

"Yeah," chimed in another. "If you know what's good for you."

Someone bumped into Gwen from behind and she looked over her shoulder to see Tobias, the baker's son.

"What's going on out there?" he asked.

"Some of the soldiers have taken an interest in Garre," Gwen replied. "Garre's angry, but I think he'll keep his temper under control."

"I can't stand those soldiers," Tobias muttered. "They think they can come to our town and do whatever they want just because they wear the king's emblem."

"As long as we stay out of their way, we don't have anything to worry about," Gwen said. "They're just following orders."

Tobias snorted but didn't say anything.

Garre was glaring daggers at the soldiers, but he stayed where he was.

"Good dog," one of the soldiers goaded. "Now lick the dirt off my boots."

"Screw off," Garre spat.

The soldier who'd spoke drew his sword and leveled the tip at Garre's throat. "What was that, dog? Did I tell you to speak?"

Silence fell over everyone in the inn. Gwen watched intently, her heart hammering in her chest with anxiety. "They can't kill someone for no reason," she whispered.

"That's what you'd think, anyway," Tobias said. "When left unchecked, that tyrant's hired hands will do anything, including murdering innocent people."

"Watch your words, boy," one of the patrons said. "You'll bring the king's wrath down on us all."

Gwen watched with bated breath, silently praying that Garre wouldn't be hurt. She wasn't friends with him, but she knew who he was, and they'd never had any issues. Even if they had, Gwen would never wish harm on anyone.

"Get to licking," the soldier demanded, lifting his boot near Garre's face. For a moment, Gwen thought he was going to lick the soldier's boot. Instead, Garre grabbed onto the soldier's leg and pulled, forcing the soldier to fall onto his back.

"Yeah!" Tobias shouted. "Give him what for!"

Gwen had a feeling something terrible was about to happen. The soldier scrambled back onto his feet and kicked Garre in the face. Garre crumbled backward awkwardly, his legs tucked under his body.

"Gods," Gwen said, flinching and looking at Tobias.

"Someone has to do something," Tobias said. "They're going to kill him."

"Don't say that," Gwen replied.

Tobias stared at her, jaw clenched. "No more," he said.

Before Gwen could figure out what he meant, Tobias drew a dagger and pushed past her. He sprinted toward the soldier that had kicked Garre and leaped onto his back, driving the small blade into the soldier's chest.

The world froze.

Gwen's eyes widened in horror and surprise. She screamed, and the world began moving again, but now it was a blur. The other soldiers grabbed Tobias and forced him to the ground, wrenching his dagger away. The soldier he'd attempted to stab was uninjured.

"Some dogs don't understand loyalty," he said, then lifted his sword up threateningly. With a sudden grunt, he staggered forward as Garre pushed him from behind. Another soldier drew his sword and thrust it into Garre's back.

Gwen stepped back from the door, shaken. Garre screamed and fell to the ground, writing in the dirt. There was confusion among the rest of the soldiers as they glanced at each other with uncertainty. Tobias broke free of the men holding him and sprinted to the left, running down the alley beside the inn.

The apparent leader threw his arms up. "Don't just stand there, get him!"

The others chased after Tobias and Gwen quietly shut the door and returned to the bar. The patrons slowly went back to their tables, but the mood had changed. The bard had stopped playing his music and the conversations became muted.

Gwen wrung her hands together nervously, not knowing what she could do to help Garre. Should she help him? What if he had done something to warrant the interest of the soldiers and she wasn't privy to that knowledge? She started to head around the bar when the kitchen door flung open and Tobias ran in, followed by Boris, Gwen's father.

"What's going on?" Boris demanded.

"I need somewhere to hide," Tobias replied. He looked around the inn, frantic. Gwen thought he looked like a frightened deer, ready to flee at any moment.

Boris looked around the room, noting the patrons, then grabbed onto the edge of the bar. "Help me, will you?"

Tobias grabbed the other end and, together, they heaved the stout wooden structure forward. Gwen was surprised to see a trap door hidden in the floor.

Boris opened the small door and motioned to the darkness within. "Go," he said. "Hurry."

Tobias didn't question the order and hurried down into the hidden space. Boris closed the door and tried to move the bar back into place, but it was too heavy. He looked at Gwen, then changed his mind and turned to the customers.

"Someone give me a hand!"

A few people leaped to their feet to help and, within a few moments, the bar was back in place.

"Father," Gwen said softly, following him into the kitchen. "You never told me about that door."

"Forget that you ever saw it," Boris replied, washing his hands off in a bucket of clean water. He went back to preparing meals as if nothing had happened.

Gwen watched her father work, wondering why his demeanor had changed so suddenly. There was something he wasn't telling her, that much was obvious. There was shouting in the common room and Gwen rushed out of the kitchen. The soldiers had entered the inn and were harassing the customers.

"Gentlemen," Gwen greeted loudly, offering the largest smile she could muster. "Drinks?"

"We're looking for a criminal," one of them said. Gwen turned her attention to him and recognized him as the leader of the group from outside.

"I don't think I've seen anyone shady in here, but I'll help if I can," Gwen said cheerily. She was surprised her voice hadn't cracked.

"This person is an enemy of the king. He's dangerous and we need to remove him from the streets. He's about my height and build, with black hair."

Gwen put a puzzled look on her face and slowly shook her head. "I can't say I've seen anyone like that in here. Would you like a drink while your men ask my customers?"

"I'd love one, but I must refuse. I'm on duty."

"Right. Can't have you out there staggering around on the job." Gwen laughed. The soldier didn't share her mirth. The kitchen door opened as Boris came out, carrying a tray full of food. The soldier jumped, obviously startled, then calmed when he saw there was no threat.

"Evening," Boris greeted as he passed them, delivering the food to a table by the windows.

"If you see anyone matching the description, please report it to the local constabulary. They'll get word to us."

"I will," Gwen replied.

The soldier turned his back to Gwen, and she noticed the uneasiness of the customers. Most were minding their own business, but a few people were staring death at the soldiers. Boris returned to the bar and the lead soldier stopped him.

"Are you the owner?"

"I am," Boris replied, offering a grin. "It's a humble place, but it's served me well."

"It's a dump," the soldier grunted. "I've also heard that it's a den of protection for the king's enemies."

Boris looked pained. "I hope no one questions my devotion to the king," he said. "I've been a staunch supporter all my years."

The soldier stared at Boris intently, then nodded, seeming satisfied.

"Anything?" the soldier asked his men.

"Nothing," someone answered.

"Let's go, then." The lead soldier looked from Boris to Gwen, then headed for the door. His men followed after him and they exited the inn. Gwen sighed in relief and leaned over the bar.

"That was close," she whispered.

There was a pounding noise at the door and Gwen realized that the soldiers were securing it so that no one could leave.

"Father, what's happening? Why did he say we're hiding enemies here?"

Boris suddenly looked older to her. Deep lines spread across his face and there were bags under his eyes.

"There are things I haven't told you because I wanted to keep you safe," Boris replied.

The customers of the inn began to panic and started kicking at the door. A few others picked up chairs and broke some of the windows, but they were greeted with flaming torches that were thrown into the inn. People scattered out of the way, knocking over tables and spilling drinks. Alcohol hit the torches and flames spread across the floor.

"We've got to get out of here!" Gwen shouted.

Boris grabbed her hand and led her through the kitchen to the backdoor, but when he pushed on it, it didn't budge.

"They've blocked us in," Boris said grimly.

"We're broke," Jayde said, casting a baleful glance at Lochlan, the ship's pilot.

"We'll find another job," Gavin replied. He was always defending Loch, and Jayde hated him for it. Perhaps hate was too strong a word. She turned her fiery gaze on Gavin and frowned. Fine, she didn't *hate* him. But it really annoyed her when he stood in the way of Loch taking responsibility for his mistakes.

"You know, we wouldn't have to find another job if Loch could stick to the plan and quit screwing anything that walks on two legs."

"That's not fair, Jayde, and you know it."

Loch stood up from his chair and crossed his arms. Jayde turned to face him, and they engaged in a silent stare-down. Her green eyes bored into his blue ones. Neither one would give in, and eventually, Gavin stepped between them and smiled at Jayde.

"Come on. We both know that Loch is never going to change, so we might as well accept the fact that he's going to screw us out of a few jobs."

"Yeah, literally," Jayde muttered. "I'll be in my bunk."

She stormed off to her personal quarters, wondering for the thousandth time why she continued to put up with Loch's constant stupidity. It was like he didn't use his brain sometimes and let his second head do all the thinking. They were so close to getting a huge payday, and yet again, Loch had ruined it. The lord of a small planet had hired them to clear out a gang that had taken up residence in his city. While the rest of the crew had been doing just that, Loch had snuck away with the lord's daughter.

A servant had caught them and immediately informed her master. If it wasn't for Jayde's quick-thinking and their even quicker escape, the lord would have executed them all. As it was, Jayde wasn't sure that they had gotten away without repercussion. The rear sensors on the ship hadn't detected pursuit, but that didn't mean they were home free just yet.

Jayde entered her personal quarters and shut the door behind her. She stared at her desk, debating on whether or not she should drink a small glass of Erillian wine. It always helped calm her anger. She was fuming. Loch had managed to really screw them over on this job. Their pockets were empty and her ship needed some work, not to mention they hadn't found a high paying job in months.

She sighed and walked over to the window and stared out at the stars. The vast black landscape stretched as far as she could see. The few stars that burned on the fringe of civilization sputtered and glowed dimly.

"Even the stars are dying out here," Jayde muttered aloud.

If they couldn't find a decent gig soon, she would be forced to land on some god-forsaken outpost until she could afford to refuel the ship. When she was young and wished to see the universe, she never thought it would be in a dilapidated ship with a crew of misfits. Hell, she never thought she'd be a mercenary either, but here she was. Captain Jayde Thrin of the *Determination*.

She snorted and turned from the window just as a massive jolt rocked the ship and pitched it roughly to the side. Everything on her desk slid off the smooth polished surface and crashed to the floor. The whole vessel groaned and Jayde thought she could hear an explosion in a distant part of the ship. She staggered into the hall, stepping over fallen items on her way out. The ship jolted again and she had to throw herself bodily against a wall to keep from tumbling to the floor.

The emergency siren blared overhead, followed by Loch calling her to the bridge. If he was calling for her, then there was a serious problem. He might be a worthless womanizer, but he was a damn good pilot. Jayde hurried down the hall to the bridge, barely pausing long enough for the doors to open.

"Blast it, what's going on in here—"

The words died on her lips as she surveyed the scene. Gavin was barely standing. He was holding onto a console, struggling to keep his balance. Loch was feverishly tapping buttons on the ship's control panel and cursing vehemently. The siren continued to blare loudly, and Jayde had all she could take.

"Turn that damn thing off!"

"I'm trying," Loch shouted. "We've been hit by something and our shields are down."

"Great! They haven't finished charging yet?"

"Not quite. They're at sixty percent." Loch tapped the screen with one finger. "Sixty-five," he corrected.

"That'll have to do," Jayde said. "Turn them on."

"Aye, Captain," Loch grunted.

A few seconds later, the ship began to hum as the shields kicked on. Loch managed to straighten the ship and Jayde sat in the chair beside him and checked the rear sensors. Not far behind them, a sleek Inquisitor ship was closing the distance. Jayde ground her teeth in anger and looked at Loch.

"Nice," she muttered. "Real nice."

Loch peered at the screen and his eyes widened in surprise. "To be fair, his daughter came onto me. I hadn't even noticed her until she—"

"I don't care," Jayde interrupted. "What's done is done. But if we survive, you'll be lucky if I don't turn you in to the Convocation and collect on your bounties."

Jayde smirked as Loch immediately stopped arguing with her. His warrants with the Convocation were a sore spot. Normally, Jayde wouldn't use that weapon against him, but she was furious with him for messing up this time. They desperately needed a payday. Now they weren't just broke, they were being hunted down by the local authorities.

"We're getting a communication request," Loch said.

"Put it through," Jayde replied.

She sat up straight in her chair. Loch tapped a button on the console and the large screen that hung awkwardly above the observation deck window flickered to life and the familiar face of Lord Rasking greeted them. Jayde groaned inwardly but put on a face of bravado.

"Lord Rasking," Jayde said.

"Mercenary scum," Rasking replied. "I find it so enjoyable that I found you with your pants down, so to speak. I'll make this easy for you. Let us board you without a fight and we'll kill you and your crew quickly."

Jayde laughed in response. "Come on, Rasking. This is the crew of the *Determination*. We don't do anything easy around here. I'll tell you what. Run with your tail tucked between your legs and I won't blast your hide to dust particles immediately. I'll give you a head start."

Rasking's face scrunched into a snarl. "The only one getting blasted to pieces is going to be you." He turned to someone offscreen and ordered them to fire. The *Determination* shuddered as a barrage of laser cannon fire blasted into the side of the ship. Jayde felt a slight tremor under her boots as the shields took the brunt of the attack. She slammed a fist onto the console, ending the video feed of Rasking's ugly smile.

"Shields down to forty-five percent!" Loch shouted.

"It's time to show this petulant lord who he's messing with," Jayde said. She pressed a button on the screen and leaned forward to speak into the microphone.

"McCready, get to the gunnery bay and return fire with the plasma turrets. I want that ship burnt to a crisp!"

Jayde hoped the old grizzled veteran wasn't asleep or passed out drunk. A few moments later, scattered bolts of light filled the sky and struck the Inquisitor ship head-on. The enemy ship's defenses glowed red under the assault.

Although the *Determination* was a cargo ship, it was equipped with the latest plasma cannons for self-defense. Jayde had learned long ago that space was, for lack of a better phrase, the wild frontier. Pirates roamed the black ocean of space, looting and pillaging anyone they came across.

"Gavin, get down there and assist McCready. If we can't get a hit on their ship, we're going to be in serious trouble."

The ship's navigator sprinted off to obey and Jayde turned her attention to the console. The shields were close to failing and their fuel was running low. She knew they had enough to possibly get them to a recharge outpost, but it wouldn't be very far from their current position. Unless they were able to maim the Inquisitor vessel, it wouldn't be much of an escape.

A second volley of laser blasts left the *Determination* and struck Lord Rasking's ship. McCready's deep laughter came roaring through the comms speaker.

"We're about to have an opening in their defenses," the veteran said. "I'm going to light him up!"

Jayde had a sudden trepidation about possibly injuring Lord Rasking. He was a member of the Convocation, after all. The fact that he had threatened to kill her and her crew, however, gave her the boost she needed to push that fear away.

"Take it when you see it," she ordered.

"Is that the best idea?" Loch asked.

Jayde ignored him. He had some nerve asking a question like that. Why hadn't he asked himself that before gallivanting with Rasking's daughter? *Bastard,* she thought.

"Call the engine room," Jayde said.

Loch did as she requested. There was a short delay, then Klaus's voice crackled through the speaker.

"I've got some issues down here. Can I get back to you?"

There was a noise that sounded like an explosion, followed by some incoherent shouts, then the audio cut off. Jayde glanced at Loch. Her face remained impassive, but she was sure he could see the uncertainty in her eyes. She gave Loch a slight nod to let him know she had everything under control, then turned to look out the window and spotted Raking's vessel turning in an attempt to flee.

"I don't think so," she muttered. "McCready, hit that ship with everything you've got."

A rain of plasma blasts fell onto the Inquisitor ship, causing multiple explosions to erupt along the vessel. Jayde watched with grim satisfaction as Raking's ship lit up with flames. And then it exploded, sending debris flying in every direction. A shower of metal shrapnel struck the Determination's shield and bounced off, floating lazily through space.

The sudden realization that they had just killed a member of the Convocation made Jayde's stomach drop. Loch wouldn't be the only one with warrants now.

"Get us out of here," she ordered Loch. "Now."

"On it," he answered.

Jayde left the chair and headed for the lift. She needed to see what the commotion was in the engine room. It was a welcome distraction from the fear.

"What was I thinking?" she berated herself. "Now Rasking is dead and I'm screwed. We're all screwed."

The lift came to a stop and Jayde could smell smoke. She hurried down the hall and practically leaped down the short stairwell into the engine room. Now she didn't just smell smoke, she saw it. Black clouds were billowing off one of the engines. Klaus stood nearby, spraying foam onto the flames. The ship's mechanic managed to kill the fire, but Jayde could see the damage was done.

"What happened?" she asked.

Klaus whirled to face her. "You scared the hell out of me! Announce yourself next time, will you?"

"Will do," Jayde replied. "Sorry."

Klaus shook his head and set the fire extinguisher down. He tilted his head to either side, stretching his neck muscles.

"Something hit us hard, which caused a load of debris to land on the engine. I tried to remove it, but the weight of it all crushed the casing and broke the engine wall. We're lucky it didn't simply explode and destroy the entire ship."

"That's good news," Jayde said. "Is it fixable?"

"Not with what we've got onboard. We need to stop somewhere. The other engine wasn't damaged, but it's not going to be able to power the entire ship."

"Great. Let me know if anything changes down here."

Klaus grunted in reply and Jayde went back to the lift. Their already bad situation had just gotten worse.

About the Author

Richard Fierce is a dynamic voice in the realm of fantasy, weaving tales that transport readers to worlds beyond imagination. His journey as a wordsmith began in childhood, but it was in 2007 that he took the plunge into the world of publishing. Since then, Richard has enchanted readers with multiple novels and short stories, showcasing his versatility and creativity.

In the year 2000, Richard Fierce earned the esteemed title of Poet of the Year for his captivating poem, "The Darkness." This early recognition hinted at the depth and artistry that would define his future literary endeavors.

Beyond the written word, Richard is a co-founder of the Acworth Book Festival, a significant literary event held in Acworth, Georgia. This initiative reflects his commitment to fostering a vibrant literary community and celebrating the written word.

A resilient spirit, Richard transitioned from a career in retail to the dynamic tech industry, finding new inspiration and challenges in the world of technology when he's not immersed in crafting fantastical tales.

In his personal life, Richard is a family man, navigating the joys and challenges of marriage and parenting. With three step-daughters (pray for him), three grandchildren, a menagerie of four dogs (his beloved huskies!), and a ferret, his home is a lively haven that resembles a bustling zoo.

Richard's enduring love for fantasy was sparked in high school when a friend's mother gifted him a copy of *Dragons of Spring Dawning* by Margaret Weis and Tracy Hickman.

This transformative experience ignited a passion that has since shaped his literary career, inspiring him to create worlds where dragons soar, and adventures unfold. As readers delve into Richard Fierce's works, they embark on thrilling journeys through the fantastical landscapes born of his vivid imagination.